THE
THIRTEEN
DAYS OF
CHRISTMAS

For the Second day of Christmas

THE THIRTEEN DAYS OF CHRISTMAS

JENNY OVERTON

Illustrated by
Shirley Hughes

OXFORD
UNIVERSITY PRESS

OXFORD
UNIVERSITY PRESS

Great Clarendon Street, Oxford OX2 6DP
Oxford University Press is a department of the University of Oxford.
It furthers the University's objective of excellence in research, scholarship,
and education by publishing worldwide in

Oxford   New York

Auckland   Cape Town   Dar es Salaam   Hong Kong   Karachi
Kuala Lumpur   Madrid   Melbourne   Mexico City   Nairobi
New Delhi   Shanghai   Taipei   Toronto

With offices in

Argentina   Austria   Brazil   Chile   Czech Republic   France   Greece
Guatemala   Hungary   Italy   Japan   Poland   Portugal   Singapore
South Korea   Switzerland   Thailand   Turkey   Ukraine   Vietnam

Oxford is a registered trade mark of Oxford University Press
in the UK and in certain other countries

First published by Faber and Faber Ltd 1972
First published by Oxford University Press 2002
First published in this edition 2013

British Library Cataloguing in Publication Data

Data available

ISBN: 978-0-19-273543-0

1 3 5 7 9 10 8 6 4 2

Printed in Great Britain
Paper used in the production of this book is a natural,
recyclable product made from wood grown in sustainable forests
The manufacturing process conforms to the environmental
regulations of the country of origin

*To Sally
who read it first
and Robert
who married her*

Acknowledgements

The carol *Susanni* was collated by Percy Dearmer and is No. 118 in *The Oxford Book of Carols* by Percy Dearmer, R. Vaughan Williams, and Martin Shaw, published in 1928 by the Oxford University Press. I am grateful for permission to reproduce four verses from it. I have also used *The Oxford Book of Carols* as the source for my quotations, in whole or in part, from the following carols: *This Endris Night* (No. 39), *Lullay My Liking* (No. 182), the *Coventry Carol* (No. 22), the *Wassail Song* (Nos. 15 and 16), *My Dancing Day* (No. 71), and *Adam Lay Ybounden* (No. 180).

The ballad *St Stephen and Herod*, which I have altered slightly, appears in its fifteenth-century form as No. 22 in *English and Scottish Popular Ballads* edited by Helen Child Sargent and George Lyman Kittredge from the collection of Francis James Child and published in 1904 by George G. Harrap & Co. Ltd, and in a modernized form on page 37 of Part IV of *Young Pegasus*, an anthology of verse arranged by A. A. Le M. Simpson and published in 1936 by G. Bell & Sons Ltd.

My source for the carol *A Merry Christmas* was the BBC Radio booklet *Singing Together* published in the autumn of 1965 by the British Broadcasting Corporation.

I am grateful to all these publishers for their kindness and helpfulness.

J. M. M. O.

Note

Some of the Christmas customs which the Kitsons keep in the story are still kept today. Some used to be kept but have now been abandoned. And some were kept only in this one town, on this one Christmas.

CALENDAR

1

St Nicholas's Day

When Prudence Kitson asked her father what he would like for Christmas, he sighed and said, 'A husband for your sister.' Her brothers, James and Christopher, agreed with him. Their elder sister, Annaple, had looked after the family ever since Mama had died. She was charming and pretty and well-meaning, but she was also a very bad cook. She forgot the pie in the oven or the stew on the fire so often that dinner was burnt five days out of seven. Sometimes she even forgot what she was making, and put sugar in the meat pasties, or stewed the pears in vinegar, or tied the cake mixture in a cloth and boiled it over the fire. But although she was hopelessly vague in the kitchen, she was very brisk everywhere else; much too brisk for the family's comfort. 'James, have you made your bed? Pru, have you mended your hem? Christopher, your hair needs cutting. Papa, give me your coat, I must let out the buttons, you're beginning to put on weight.'

'I do wish she'd get married,' Christopher said crossly, stamping into the parlour after Annaple had sat him in a kitchen chair and pruned his fringe till his forehead felt cold. 'She's pretty enough—isn't she? She's as pretty as the Verney girl who got married last week.'

'Francis *wants* to marry her. So he says.' James looked up from the model ship he was making. 'He says that if she marries him she'll never have to cook a meal again. He's got enough money to pay for a cook and a housekeeper and probably half a dozen serving maids as well.'

2

'I know. And she says she likes him. Well, why won't she marry him, then?'

Prudence said, 'She thinks he isn't romantic enough. Too unimaginative, she says. Too solemn.'

'*Romantic*,' Christopher said scornfully. Annaple's fanciful ways were a great nuisance to her family. She bought a harp and sat on the window sill twanging it, singing in a small flat voice and breaking her fingernails on the gilded strings. She sighed over pear blossom in the spring, ate strawberries even though they brought her out in a rash, cooed over babies, fussed about wearing gloves to church, and wasted time embroidering flowers on a useless strip of ivory silk which had taken her three years already. She plaited her hair like a goose-girl's, stuck wilting daisies in it, and talked about the simple pleasures of country life although she had never so much as milked a cow: 'Making butter in the dairy, picking lavender, herding the geese across the fields, feeding lambs, long evenings by the fire with your patchwork—'

'P'rhaps if Francis bought a farm—' Christopher began, remembering this.

'I don't believe that would help at all,' Prudence said. 'There's too much work and mud and compost on a real farm.'

'He ought to do something—well, fanciful,' James agreed. 'Like sending her an armful of pear blossom. Or buying a flute and coming to sing under her window one night.'

The doorbell rang and Christopher leant out of the window to see who it was. 'It *is* Francis.'

'Run down and let him in, Kit,' Prudence said.

'But it's Nan he's come to see.'

'I know, but perhaps we could give him some advice. After all, we do know what Nan is like—'

'Only too well,' Christopher said bitterly. 'I suppose he really does want to marry her?'

'He says he does,' Prudence said.

Christopher clattered downstairs, and in a few minutes reappeared with Francis Vere, who had brought flowers for Annaple, as he did on every possible occasion, and pokes of sweets for the children. He began to talk about Annaple almost at once. 'She's so sweet-tempered. Not like Clarissa Verney.'

'She can be very finicky, you know,' James said cautiously. 'I suppose . . . I mean . . . you are quite sure you want to marry her?'

Christopher glared at him, thinking they shouldn't give Francis any let-out; but Francis said yes, he was quite sure.

'Where is she?' he asked, looking hopefully towards the door.

'In the kitchen. Throwing together a horrible St Nicholas Day cake. Listen. There's nothing we'd like more than to see Annaple get married—'

'Get married to you,' Prudence put in tactfully.

'—to you, so we thought perhaps we could give you some advice.'

'Advice?'

'Help.' Prudence looked at him, thinking of burnt beef and sagging cake and apples-in-caramel as hard as cannon balls. She said cautiously, 'You really can afford a cook, can't you?'

'A dozen cooks if she likes.'

'Well, actually it's you I was thinking of. I mean, Annaple never eats much—she thinks thin girls are more romantic—so it doesn't matter to her if things are all burnt up; but you don't want to starve—'

'If Annaple marries me, she need never even lift a

spoon again. I'll give her anything she likes,' Francis said earnestly.

'Anything at all?' Christopher asked, wanting to get it straight. 'Suppose she wanted a—a drum of her own? Or a sword? Or a trumpet? Or a *horse*?'

'Anything.'

'Including a piper?' James asked.

Francis was startled. 'Why a piper?'

'Because once she read a tale about Scotland—misty mountains and seals singing and dew on the heather— that was when she took to calling herself Annaple, all Scottish, instead of Annabel—'

'And before that it was Annick,' Christopher put in, 'because of French things being more romantic than English, and for a bit before that, it was Nancy. Could you get used to leaving, say, Nancy at breakfast and coming home to find Annette at supper? She was christened plain Anne, but it isn't fanciful enough for her.'

'And,' James said patiently, 'the girl in this tale—the Scottish tale, I mean—used to be woken at dawn by a piper playing a lament under her window. Annaple fancied that.'

'She may go on about the sunrise and the dew and the dawn chorus,' Christopher said, 'but I notice she stays in bed till past eight o'clock.'

Prudence said, 'Poor Francis won't want to hire a piper, not if he marries Annaple—*he'd* get woken up too.'

But Francis said he would provide a dozen pipers if Annaple wished. 'Only not the mountains, of course—

not unless we moved to Scotland or the Welsh border or somewhere in the North country.'

'That's a good idea,' Christopher said, feeling that even if by some miracle Annaple agreed to marry Francis, she might quite easily take time off to walk round to Lee Street each day and check on the family.

'If Annaple marries me,' Francis said firmly, 'she can have an army of pipers and a rockery full of heather plants, a row of silk dresses, flowers for her hair, a gold ring for her finger—'

'Five gold rings,' Christopher said, 'because both of Papa's brothers are clergymen, and so are three of Mama's, and they'd all want to be the one that did the marrying.'

'Five gold rings,' Francis said obediently. 'Why doesn't Annaple want to marry me?'

There was a pause.

Christopher said, 'It's a pity you're not a woodcutter or something like that. She goes on for ever about life in the greenwood—partridges for pets, you know, a handful of herbs for dinner, the sky for a roof, herding geese through the dewy grass—all that nonsense.'

'Or if you were the seventh son of a seventh son,' James said. 'Annaple's nutty on fairytales. Or a soldier, perhaps—haven't you ever heard her babbling about how romantic it would be to marry a soldier and follow the drum? She's been going on about that ever since Papa took us to watch the summer review in St Stephen's Fields.'

'She does like you, truly,' Prudence said. 'Very much. Only perhaps she'd like you a bit more if you were— well, more light-hearted. Imaginative.'

'Yes. Look. Are you going to give Annaple a Christmas present?' James asked.

'Of course. Anything she wa—'

'Well, couldn't you give her something imaginative? Original?'

'Anything—'

'What would she like, do you think?' Prudence asked her brothers.

'A trumpet,' Christopher said hopefully.

'If you can't be sensible, Kit—'

'What about a spinning wheel?' James said. 'That's very fairytale-ish. She said her favourite story was that one with the idiotish girl who couldn't guess Rumpelstiltskin's name.'

'It wasn't,' Christopher said. 'You're getting muddled. It was the one with the princess who had to make shirts out of nettles to bewitch her brothers back from being swans.'

'Whichever one it was,' Prudence said, 'don't you think a spinning wheel would be a nuisance? She'd be forever breaking the thread or pricking herself. That wretched embroidery's bad enough. And even if she did manage to spin some thread, we'd have to spend hours winding it. And then she'd knit scratchy stockings for us to wear. Don't you think a musical box would be better?'

'I don't know, Pru. We have trouble enough with that screeching harp. P'rhaps something French—'

'A cookery book,' Christopher said bitterly. 'A cookery book, an outsize egg timer, and an alarm clock.'

Francis was thinking. 'Yes, I see—' he said. 'Yes, I *do* see. A change from flowers. Yes, all right, I'll think something up.'

* * *

When Francis left, Prudence walked with him down Lee Street to the Market Place. It was choir practice night and the church door was open. 'Listen,' Prudence said suddenly. 'I thought—yes, it is, it's the opening bit of the Advent carol.'

Francis and she stood in the doorway to listen. The pipes and fiddles were playing the introduction. A boy's solitary voice lifted in the Advent carol for the coming of Christmas.

'Sheep like stones
In silent fold,
Snow like ash
Settling cold.

Walk a world
Bereft as dream,
Birdless wood,
Standing stream.

9

Bethlehem:
The children whine;
Travellers
Wait in line.

Tired men ring
The courtyard fire,
Tethered mules
Crowd the byre.

Stumble through
The cattle-pens;
Overhead
Roosting hens.

Spread with bales
The reeking floor;
Birthing bed:
Sacks and straw.

Trim the lamp;
Bemused and numb,
Watch and wait:
Soon, a son.'

Prudence said, 'I wonder if Nan's remembered to order the Christmas candle.'

Francis wasn't listening. 'Something imaginative,' he said. 'Something original. I must think this over.'

'Well, don't take too long,' Prudence said. 'It will be Christmas in no time at all now. I can never really believe it till I hear them singing the waiting carol.'

2

Christmas Eve

On Christmas Eve Annaple gave James and Christopher a couple of buckets and a bundle of rags and sent them to wash the front windows. 'We must have the house clean for Christmas.' They muttered and complained a bit, but cleaning windows outdoors was better than polishing furniture in, which was what Prudence was doing, so in the end James got the ladder and Christopher filled the buckets and they went off to do as they'd been told.

The Kitsons' house was tall and thin, two rooms to a floor and five floors high. The pantry and the kitchen in the cellarage looked out on the sunk courtyard behind the house, but the hall and the study on the ground floor looked the other way, into the street. The parlour and Papa's bedroom were on the first floor, the girls' room and the spare room were on the second, and the boys slept in the attic under the roof. Because the kitchen was below street level, the house's back door was nine feet lower than the front one.

The front door opened out of the hall on to a small stone bridge. Each house on the north side of Lee Street had its own bridge over the stream which ran down the deep stone gutter towards the Market Place. Annaple was very particular about this stream and made the boys scrub out the gutter once a week. 'In fact,' James said, as he balanced the ladder on the bridge, 'she's too particular altogether. I wonder if Francis has picked out a really imaginative present for her?'

'It'll probably be flowers, as usual. Though I did meet him in town yesterday, and he asked me to list all the things she's ever mooned over, so p'rhaps it'll be something a bit more original this time.' Christopher put his foot on the first rung. 'Mind you hold it steady, Jem. If I break my neck, it'll be Annaple's blame.'

Christopher didn't bother with the attic windows at all. He gave the girls' bedroom window a lick and a promise; skimped the window of the spare room; took a quick swipe at the parlour; and didn't even do that for Papa's bedroom. 'Papa will never notice,' he said cheerfully. 'He walks around in his own little cloud of tobacco smoke all day long.'

'You'd better do the study, though. Nan might easily check on that.'

Christopher slithered down the ladder and perched on the stone ledge where the house wall jutted out above the stream. Papa was in the study, marooned at his desk, with Annaple polishing briskly all around him and telling him it was time he got some new shirts, he really must take his shoes to the cobbler's, and oughtn't he to have his hair cut? 'It doesn't seem very fair on Francis,' Christopher said, when he had given the study windows a thorough polish, grinned at Papa, made a face at Annaple, and edged back to the bridge.

'No one can say we haven't warned him. Come on, let's slip off to the Market Place. There'll be hot chestnuts and the mummers doing their play and maybe a juggler as well.'

But Annaple opened the study window and called them back, and made them put the ladder away and empty the buckets, chop wood for the Christmas fires, sweep the courtyard and clean the shoes; and even when she did send them down to the Market—'Butter, nutmegs, goose-fat, and oranges'—she made them promise to come straight back. At last, however, when they had done the marketing and laid fresh fires and hauled up a dozen buckets of water from the well, she gave them a bundle of apples and cheese and burnt mutton pasty and sent them off to cut holly and ivy in the greenwood.

Once there, they took their time. They went deep into the wood, gathering long trails of ivy and holly branches stiff with berries. At last James stopped to hoist his bundle higher on his back, and looking around him, realized that it was growing dark. 'Kit!' he called. 'Kit, it's almost owl-light, we'd better turn back.' Christopher, who had hoped to get as far as the Keeper's cottage, glowered a bit but gave in. They turned back. The wood was dusking into darkness. They blundered on through the trees, tripping over hidden roots and stumbling into spongy pockets of leaf-mould; James began to be afraid they had lost the way altogether and was frankly relieved when at last they emerged to see St Stephen's Fields black under a sky the colour of ripe sloes, and the

15

lantern shining out from the distant Church tower. The wind was coming off the sea.

'I wish we could go the long way round, by the Eastcliff—' James began.

'What, an extra mile just to snuff at the sea? You were fretting about being late just a few minutes back.'

'Yes, I suppose so.'

They tied their bundles to a hurdle and dragged it across the fields and up the long slope to the West Gate. Candles were alight in the windows. James began to whistle *The Holly and the Ivy* and Christopher joined in with the words; he didn't have a choirboy's voice, not like Will Verney, but he sounded loud and cheerful, and a woman opened her window and threw him some

pennies. He spent them on chestnuts and barley sugar
in the Market Place, where James and he lingered for a
little while to watch the mummers.

When they got home, they found Annaple in the
kitchen, checking the Christmas stores, and Prudence
stirring a stew over the fire.

'It *was* going to be stewed apple, for pudding,'
Prudence said, when James sniffed it suspiciously, 'only
then Nan forgot, and put in onions, so then she added
rabbit pieces and some bits of spice—'

'*Spice?*'

'She had cloves in it already, for the apple, so she can't
have made it any worse. She put in the rest of the pars-
ley as well, because it seemed a pity to waste it, and then

17

some nutmeg, and then the raisins left over from the Christmas pudding.'

'You *can* get a hot Christmas dinner sent up from the Pig and Whistle,' Christopher mentioned cautiously; luckily Annaple didn't hear this.

'Prices are shocking,' she said, trying to check the bill on her fingers. 'A little bit of butter, a string of onions, some cream, a brace of rabbits, a dozen eggs, and that's the housekeeping gone. The butter we eat in this house in one week would grease a dozen maypoles. I wish we had a farm.'

'Would you really like a farm, Nan?' Christopher said hopefully. 'For Christmas, I mean?'

'Don't be silly.' Annaple counted the eggs again and could still only make it twelve. 'But things would be much cheaper if we did.'

'Why?'

'Eggs from one's own hens, milk and cream and butter from one's own cows, home-grown cabbages. And besides, think how delightful it would be, a little herd of geese, doing one's patchwork by the hearth, moonlight on the orchard, a coop of partridges, a herb garden, lambs, primroses—'

'Holy Maria, she's off again.'

'It isn't really like that,' Prudence pointed out. 'Geese hiss at you, and everything's muddy, and you have to be up at dawn—'

'And no piper to wake you up,' James put in. 'A cockerel if you're lucky, that's all.'

'But at least on a farm you could have a horse,' Christopher said longingly, switching sides for the moment.

'Horses!' Prudence stirred the stew with such vigour that it slopped over the rim and hissed in the fire. 'Great lumpy things with huge yellow teeth.'

'Oh but, Pru, think of when Papa took us to see the review,' Annaple said; she was well away now. 'The soldiers in their red coats, and the drummers, and the fifes, and those beautiful glossy horses, and all the flags flying.'

'Yes, but—'

'Battles are shocking, of course,' Annaple said, 'but in peacetime—following the drum, saluting the Colours—'

'Francis's father was a soldier,' Prudence remarked. 'Wasn't he?'

'I believe so,' Annaple said. 'Yes, I believe so. But Francis isn't interested in the army. He spends all day long in that musty counting house.'

'Well, that's quite useful in its way,' Prudence said.

'Would you like a horse for Christmas, p'rhaps?' Christopher asked Annaple. 'We could turn the wood-shed into a stable. And the courtyard's quite big really.'

'Don't be silly, Kit. Why don't you and Jem hang up the Christmas greenery?'

* * *

James and Christopher stuck holly and ivy all over the house, hung up the kissing ring, and nailed the

Christmas wreath on the front door. Out in the streets small boys were whistling for snow. Annaple dished up the stew, and afterwards they all took the taste away with the mince pies Aunt Rachel had sent round. Then they went up to the parlour and sat, waiting. Annaple fidgeted with her embroidery, setting an occasional stitch; Papa sat peacefully smoking his pipe; James rigged his model ship, Christopher played softly on his penny whistle; but Prudence did nothing at all except listen to the flap of the flames and the plucking of Annaple's needle through the silk, and strain to hear the sounds of the carol singers' approach.

'They're coming—I'm sure I heard—yes, they're coming—'

She ran to the window. The carol singers were trudging down the street. They were whistling and laughing. Someone was playing short runs on a pipe. Someone else was banging a drum.

James pushed the window open as far as it would go and they all leaned out. Prudence craned to catch the first glimpse of the Christmas cart. The candlelit windows across the street were crowded with people.

'Listen—they're coming—'

They heard the steady clopping of a horse's hooves, the rumbling of wheels over cobblestones. The cart creaked slowly into view. In it sat Mary, in her blue cloak and hood, and Joseph, holding a lantern. The cart was full of hay, thickly scattered with rosemary and bay leaves; the smell drifted up to the open windows.

The singers' voices were light and clear.

> 'This endris night
> I saw a sight,
> A star as bright as day;
> And ever among,
> A maiden sung,
> Lullay, by, by, lullay.'

Prudence sighed with pleasure. It was one of her favourite carols. Through the six succeeding verses she watched and listened until Mary's voice floated, solitary, above the singers' humming:

> 'Now sweet son, since it is come so,
> That all is at thy will,
> I pray thee grant to me a boon,
> If it be right and skill,—
> That child or man, who will or can
> Be merry on my day,
> To bliss thou bring—and I shall sing,
> Lullay, by, by, lullay.'

People began to clap, pennies rang on the cobbles, and the cart creaked on downhill.

* * *

Just before midnight, Annaple lit a taper at the fire and carried it across to the window, where the

Christmas candle stood in its special candlestick. The candle was made of the best wax, yellow and sweet-smelling, as tall as a bulrush and thicker than Prudence's wrist. Annaple bent forward, shielding the taper with her fingers, and lit the wick. The flame opened out. It would burn from Christmas Eve through the twelve holy days of Christmas to the Feast of the Three Kings.

They put on their cloaks and lit candles and went out into the night. Like everyone else in town, except the very young and the very old, they walked down to the Market Place. Sparks streamed from the torches that the older men were carrying. The candle flames dipped in a stir of air from the sea. The carol singers were still travelling round the town. Prudence could hear the creak of their chained lanterns and the sound of their voices singing up and down the streets. The fife blew shrilly, a high wintry sound, and the drum throbbed in the stillness.

* * *

When the Mass was over and they came out from church into the midwinter night, Prudence was half-asleep. The lanternlit cart was drawn up in the Market Place. Shepherds knelt around it on the cobblestones. Mary held the baby in the crook of her arm. Above the cry of a lamb, voices sang over and over in the darkness, *'Lullay, my liking, my dear son, my sweeting, lullay, my dear heart, mine own dear darling.'*

22

3

Christmas Day

Francis came to call on Christmas morning after Aunt Rachel and the uncles had come and gone. Prudence ran downstairs to let him in.

'Merry Christmas, Pru.'

'Merry Christmas, Francis.' Prudence stared at the great bundle in his arms. 'Whatever's that?'

'It's a surprise. For Annaple. I do hope she'll like it.' He looked hopefully at Prudence. 'I tried to remember everything you said.'

'Everything?' Prudence said, startled. She thought of some of the presents Christopher and James had suggested. Francis was always wholehearted. She said cautiously, 'What is it?'

'Wait and see. Or guess.'

'I can't possibly. It doesn't *look* like anything.' She gazed at it for a moment. 'It isn't a horse, anyway,' she said with relief.

'If you think Nan would like a horse, I could easily—'

'Goodness, no. I was only joking.'

They went up to the parlour. Papa was heating a poker for the punch, James and Christopher were roasting apples, and Annaple was talking about the joys of a simple Christmas. 'A sprig of holly over the door and chestnuts on the fire.'

'Sounds like a hungry Christmas to me,' Christopher said.

'Don't be so greedy. Good morning, Francis. Merry Christmas.'

'Merry Christmas, Annaple.' Francis dumped his bundle on the table. Annaple eyed it with surprise, but was too polite to comment.

Francis pulled more presents out of his pocket. 'For you, Pru—and James—and Christopher—and for you, sir.'

He had brought a musical box for Prudence, a fife for James, and a trumpet for Christopher—Annaple looked askance at these, but swallowed her comments—and a new clay pipe for Papa, who was delighted. 'How very kind of you, Francis. You must have a cup of punch.' He plunged the red-hot poker into the punch bowl and stirred vigorously. The punch hissed and foam ran down into the hearth.

'For you, Nan.' Francis pushed the parcel towards her.

'Why, Francis, thank you.' Annaple put a note of delighted surprise into her voice, as though she had only just noticed the vast untidy bundle. 'What is it? Flowers?'

Francis shook his head. Annaple began to look quite

interested. She circled the table. The parcel rustled. Annaple said, startled, 'Is it alive?' and moved back a step.

'Well, yes,' Francis said. Christopher, who had been concentrating on his trumpet, looked up in sudden interest.

'*Alive?*'

'It won't bite,' Francis said reassuringly.

Annaple, still wary but too polite to hold back, reached for a trailing end of ribbon. She pulled cautiously. The ribbons fell away and the paper crumpled. Everyone gasped. 'Holy Maria,' Papa said, swallowing a mouthful of smoke by mistake and choking over it. 'What's that?'

On the table stood a small tree in a red pot. A fat brown bird was blinking and clucking in the branches.

'It's a partridge,' Francis said, gazing hopefully at Annaple. 'And a pear tree. Only a miniature pear tree, of course, but they assured me it will flower. I thought you could put it on your windowsill, Annaple, in the moonlight—and the partridge is perfectly tame, I got it from the Keeper. It can live in the courtyard—I'll send round a coop.'

'Extraordinary,' Papa said. 'Quite extraordinary.'

He took a gulp of punch and stared at Francis as if he didn't quite believe what he was seeing. 'It's the cra— the most extraordinary present I ever saw.'

'But very original,' James said urgently.

'Very unusual.'

'Terribly imaginative.'

Annaple didn't seem to hear. She bent forward to stroke the partridge. It made small pleased clucking sounds and sidled along the branch to nibble her fingers.

'It's delightful,' she said. 'It's the most delightful present anyone ever had.'

* * *

'She was pleased,' Prudence said, as she opened the front door and Francis stepped out on to the bridge.

'She's a wonderful girl,' Francis said happily.

'She's a terrible cook.'

'Do you think she'd like another?'

'Another what?'

'Another partridge. In another pear tree.'

'*Another?*'

'You see,' Francis said diffidently, 'I'm not used to buying one of anything—not just one at a time, I mean—you get out of the way of it when the trading ships come back with a thousand bales of silk, a thousand vats of wine, a thousand bushels of wheat. So actually I got a dozen. I always do, I didn't think—'

'What a wonderful way to be,' Prudence said. 'So you've got *eleven* more partridges at home?'

'Well, yes. And eleven pear trees. I thought that perhaps I could send round one a day. And perhaps,' he said, 'some other little thing as well?'

4

St Stephen's Day

St Stephen's Day was the only day of the year on which all the boys in the town were up well before seven. It was still dark when the streets rang with their shrill hopeful whistling for snow. A snowball fight was the best of all the Stephen's Day battles; they would come stumbling home from it clogged and choked and drenched with snow, breathless and frozen, their eyes stinging and their knuckles raw. But this year the stream ran freely down the gutter and the wind blew from the south-west, smelling of the fields; there was no real hope of snow today.

Prudence and Annaple were woken before first light by the sound of boys whistling and crowing like cocks and singing the Stephen's Day carol.

'St Stephen was a clerk in King Herod's hall,
And served him of bread and cloth, as every
  King befall.

Stephen out of kitchen came, with boar's head
  in hand;
He saw a star was fair and bright over Bethlem stand.'

Prudence yawned and said, 'I wonder who the soloists
are?' and Will Verney's voice sang up from the street:

' "I forsake thee, King Herod, and thy works all;
There is a child in Bethlem born is better than
  we all." '

Prudence padded to the window and looked out in the
hope of seeing a star. The small yellow lights of the
lanterns bobbed cheerfully down the street, and a louder
deeper voice roared out to answer Will's:

' "What aileth thee, Stephen? What is thee befall?
Lacketh thee either meat or drink in King Herod's
  hall?"

"Lacketh me neither meat nor drink in King Herod's
  hall;
There is a child in Bethlem born is better than
  we all."

"That is all so true, Stephen, all so true, iwis,
As this cock'rel crow shall, that lieth here in my dish."

That word was not so soon said, that word in that
  hall,
The cock'rel crew "Christ is born" among the lords all.'

Annaple yawned and turned over. 'You'll catch your death standing there,' she murmured. 'Come back to bed.'

> ' "Rise up, my tormentors, lay to and all be one,
> And lead Stephen out of this town and stone him with stone!"
>
> Took he Stephen and stoned him in the way;
> And therefore is his even on Christ's own day.'

There was an outburst of thumping on the Kitsons' front door. 'Come on, cowardies! We'll break your bones, we'll crack your ribs, we'll tan your hide—'

A window banged open overhead. Christopher shouted the traditional answer. 'Sticks and stones may break our bones but words can never harm us! Wait, Will, we're coming down—just a minute—hurry *up*, Jem—'

There was a new burst of jeering and cockcrowing. Annaple thumped over in bed. 'Surely they needn't make so much noise,' she said crossly.

Prudence giggled and reached out for her wrapper. 'I almost wish I was going too.'

'Then try remembering the year James broke his collar bone. The whole thing's a scandal—rowdy, vulgar, savage—Papa shouldn't allow it.'

James and Christopher clattered down the stairs. The front door slammed, there were shouts and whistles in the street, a splash as someone fell into the stream, a roar of laughter; then the sound of running feet, more doors banging, and the traditional shouts fading in the distance.

'And last year Will Verney turned his ankle and couldn't set foot to ground for six weeks after,' Annaple went on. 'And the year before that—'

'It's part of Christmas, Nan. It's a tradition.'

'Traditions should be romantic—like Churching Day, or Wassailing, or Dancing Day, or New Year. They'll come limping home with their clothes in rags, covered in mud, skinned, bruised, with black eyes and bloody noses and feverish with excitement. It shouldn't be allowed,' Annaple said stubbornly; and turned over and buried her face in the pillow, plainly intending to sleep for at least another hour.

* * *

When James and Christopher came stumbling home, hot and excited and smeared with mud, they found Annaple counting out Christmas boxes in the kitchen. 'The butcher, the baker, the candlestick maker—oh dear, there's no end to it. I wish I were rich.'

'Really rich, Nan?' Christopher said, yawning hugely and lolling against the table. 'As rich as Francis?'

'You don't know what you're talking about. The cobbler, the keeper, the chimney stack sweeper.' Annaple clinked sixpences crossly. 'You're both filthy, just as I said you would be—Are you hurt?'

'No, of course not.'

Annaple looked them both over suspiciously, and having checked that they were indeed unhurt, went back to counting out the money. 'The draper, the ditcher, the petticoat stitcher. The grocer, the grinder, the clock-and-watch winder. Go and wash. Properly. I shall check.'

'But we're hungry. We've had a very wearing morning,' Christopher said persuasively. 'Couldn't we have breakfast first?'

But Annaple had been annoyed by his remark about Francis. 'No,' she said. 'I'll cook your breakfast when you're clean and ready for it, not before. The tiler, the thatcher, the rat-and-mouse catcher. There's a tub of water out in the yard. Leave your jackets, your shirts, and your stockings on that chair.'

'Water?' Christopher said cautiously. 'Hot water, do you mean?'

'I do not. Straight from the well, I drew it myself. There's a potful of hot water on the hook over the fire, you can take that.'

'But, Nan, that'll hardly take the chill off.'

'Think yourselves lucky it will do that,' Annaple retorted. She had spent two hours imagining all the injuries her brothers might have suffered, down in St Stephen's Fields, and now that they were home safe and sound, could take out her anxieties on them. 'Hurry up,' she said crisply; and went back to her counting.

James looked at Christopher, shrugged, dropped his torn jacket on the chair and pulled off his old flannel shirt. Christopher sighed heavily and began to undo his buttons. The doorbell rang. Prudence, who had been peeling apples by the fire, ran upstairs to answer it. A messenger was standing on the bridge, peering round an armful of partridge-in-pear-tree. 'For Miss Annaple Kitson.'

'Goodness.' Prudence stared—not at the expected potted pear complete with partridge, but at the cage swinging from the messenger's thumb. It was a gilded cage, very fanciful, with oak leaves at each corner, a pineapple on top, and a miniature portcullis instead of a door. Inside were two turtle doves, bowing and crooning.

'And a letter for Miss Prudence Kitson.'
Prudence opened her letter.

St Stephen's Day.

My dear Prudence,

I trust you will approve the Doves. I am assured
they are exceedingly romantic. Wld Nan care to
make a short sea voyage today? If she is not wishful, James and Christopher might care to come
in her stead. I present my Respectful Greetings to
yr Father, and my Thanks for the kind
Entertainment yesterday. My compliments,

FRANCIS VERE.

If James and Christopher are wishful to come,
I suggest fishing rods wld be appropriate, but do
not proffer the Invitation, Pru, until Nan has
declared her unwillingness. Yrself exceedingly
welcome either way. F.

'Look, Nan,' Prudence said.
Annaple was delighted. 'Oh, such pretty little things.
We must hang them up in the parlour window. Look,
Papa, aren't they charming?'
'What in the world are those?'
'Doves, of course. Turtle doves.'

'They're like the ones Joseph carries into the Church on Churching Day,' Prudence said.

Annaple was reading the streamer attached to the bars. '*For the second day of Christmas.* How sweet of Francis. I must write and thank him at once.'

Prudence and James and Christopher looked triumphantly at one another, and even Papa looked pleased.

'Nan—' Prudence said, remembering, and thinking this was as good a moment as any to break the news, 'Nan, he sent something else as well. I'll fetch it.'

She brought the partridge downstairs, eyeing Annaple doubtfully; but Annaple was delighted. 'He's sent a mate, how thoughtful of him. I was afraid Polly might be lonely.'

'Extraordinary sympathies you have,' Papa said. 'Double trouble. But I suppose if you have one partridge, you may as well have a pair. Why are you looking like that, Pru?'

'Nothing,' Prudence said hastily.

James said, 'Has he sent another pear tree too?'

'What?—oh, yes. In a green pot, this time.'

'I'll put the trees in the windows on either side of the front door,' Annaple decided. 'And when it gets warmer, we can put them out on the bridge.'

Prudence explained about the sea trip. Annaple said it was very kind of Francis, very thoughtful, but she had a great deal to do, she would prefer to stay at home. Prudence said she would stay too—like Annaple, she was always sick at sea—and did James and Christopher want to go fishing?

The boys were delighted. 'I'll get the rods,' Christopher said, diving for the stairs.

'You'll go straight outside and wash,' Annaple said firmly.

'But, Nan, we'll catch our deaths—'

'Either you go and wash, or I send a note round to Francis saying you won't be able to go sailing today. Wash your hair too—it's caked with mud. Duck your heads under and rub the soap well in.'

They were damp and clean and shivering when at last she let them back into the kitchen.

'If we die of a fever, it'll be your blame, Nan,' Christopher said, making straight for the fire.

'Did you empty the tub and scour it out?'

'Yes, yes,' James said, struggling into his clean shirt. 'When will breakfast be ready?'

'In five minutes.' Annaple counted the breakfast eggs into the pot. 'I wish we had a hen,' she said. 'When Christmas is over, we must get a couple.'

* * *

'All the way to *France* and back?' Prudence said enviously, staring at James, who gave an enormous yawn and stretched his hands to the fire. 'Truly, Jem? You're not making it up to tease me?'

James grinned and shook his head. 'Where's the poker, Pru?' he said. 'Stir up the coals.'

'I'll do my best, but the fire's nearly dead. We kept thinking you'd be home any minute, but it got later and later, and Nan got worrieder and crosser, and when it came to midnight even Papa began to sound anxious—'

'I know—Francis was very apologetic. He said he'd come round in the morning and explain.'

'It's morning now, nearly,' Prudence said.

She went to the window and looked out. The lantern shone in the church tower to guide the fishermen home, but the rest of the town was in darkness. Everyone was asleep: Papa had taken himself off to bed, saying he would hear explanations in the morning, and Annaple had gone up too, pushing Christopher ahead of her—a docile Christopher, almost asleep on his feet—and telling James and Prudence to finish their milk, cover the fire, and come to bed. 'We're the only people awake,' Prudence said, yawning. 'In all the town, only us.' But even as she said it, she heard footsteps on the cobbles and saw the glow of a lantern at the far end of the street. The night watchman was making his rounds.

'Past three o'clock,' he was chanting as he walked. 'Past three o'clock, and a cold frosty morning. Past three o'clock, good morrow, masters all—' As he passed below the parlour window, he chanted the special verse which belonged to the Christmas season: 'Born is a baby, gentle as may be. Past three o'clock, and all's well.'

Prudence turned back into the room to see James nodding by the fire. 'You'd better get to bed,' she said.

'In a minute.' He seemed to wake up a little. 'We really

must see that Nan marries Francis, he'd make the most wonderful brother-in-law. He was as casual as if . . . as if he was saying, let's go to the Market.'

'What was it like, Jem?'

James thought for a moment. 'First of all we saw this thin bluish line—we'd been sailing for some time by then—at least, it didn't *seem* long, but it must have been hours—and Francis said there it is, that's the coast of France. And then he said, would you like to go ashore? So of course we said yes. And as we stood in to the land—'

'As you did what?'

'—as we went nearer—well, it heaved up into cliffs, proper cliffs, though lower than the Eastcliff, of course—and then they opened out, like an estuary, and we sailed upriver till we came to a town—like ours, in a way, but different, you could tell at once that it wasn't England—the church tower was different, for one thing, it had arches in it, little round arches you could see the sky through—and all the houses were flat against the street, you couldn't see any gardens, and there were little paved squares. So anyway, we moored, and then Francis marched off to find the Mayor, who was a very merry sort of man, not a bit like ours—round and red, like the Man in the Moon. And Francis pulled out his purse and began to put money on the table—acting it out, you see, as if he was buying something. And the Mayor looked a bit puzzled at first, but then he started nodding away, so then Francis made clucking noises, and

I pretended to search for eggs, and Kit went cockledoodledoo, cockledoodledoo, over and over, and strutted
around—and suddenly the Mayor seemed to realize
what we meant, and he called in a servant and rattled
away in French—'

'But what *did* you mean?' Prudence said.

'Hens, of course. You see, Francis said he must take
Nan back a present, and what would she like, and I
remembered what she said this morning about getting a
couple of hens—you know how she babbles on about
baby chicks and the joys of hunting for newlaid eggs in
the straw and all that nonsense—so *anyway*, the Mayor
beckoned us into the kitchen, and his wife brought out
some bread, the most peculiar bread in long thin loaves
like sticks, yards and yards of it, and a big squishy

cheese, and some wonderful soup, without stewed apples in it or anything crazy like that—and then there was the most enormous row in the courtyard, a great crowd of people with hens tucked under their arms, and all the hens were squawking like mad, and the people were chattering in French at the tops of their voices, and there were feathers everywhere, the air was full of them—you remember when Annaple was turning the mattress and it ripped and she disappeared in a great cloud of feathers? Like that—'

'Jem—how *many* hens did Francis buy?'

James grinned. 'Hundreds—no, no, Pru, there's no need to look so horrified. Not hundreds. Two and a half dozen.'

Prudence counted on her fingers. 'That's—that's *thirty*!'

'I know. Francis didn't turn a hair.'

'Perhaps not, but Papa will turn every hair he has.' Prudence eyed her brother suspiciously. 'Surely you could have stopped him?'

'I suppose I could,' James admitted cheerfully, 'in fact, I was going to, but then I thought of how cross Nan was this morning, pushing us outside to wash in all that icy water, and I decided she could just put up with it.'

'She worries about you on Stephen's Day—'

'I know that, of course I do, but she could have let us wash in warm water in the kitchen, couldn't she? And anyway, Francis doesn't seem to think he's got value for money unless he buys at least a dozen of whatever it is.

I can't think how he restrained himself to just two partridges and two pear trees and two turtle doves.'

'Well, actually—'

'And he bought some wine too, as we were in France, six dozen bottles of it, think of that, and about a mile of bread, for us to eat on the way back, and a whole cheese the size of a cartwheel, and a dozen pots of honey. So we carried everything down to the jetty and loaded the boat, and then a fiddler appeared and started playing, and people started dancing, and someone opened the wine. It's lucky the wind veered or we wouldn't have been back tonight at all.'

'Annaple isn't pleased with Francis. She thought you were all drowned.'

'She won't be pleased when she sees our clothes either. They're stiff with salt.'

'She certainly won't be pleased when she finds thirty chickens on the doorstep,' Prudence said despairingly. 'It'll undo all the good we've managed to do. She was delighted with the partridges and the pear trees, really delighted, and she was cooing away this evening— before she began to worry about you, that is—and saying how romantic turtle doves were, and how considerate Francis was, and she would never have thought he could be so imaginative.'

'It's not as bad as that,' James said. 'Promise you, Pru. Francis began to wonder if perhaps thirty chickens all at once would be too much for her, so he said he'd send round three, and if she liked them he'd send the rest, and if not he'd give them away.' He yawned and stretched. 'It was glorious sailing back in the dark—we sang all the way, and Francis showed me how to steer by the stars—he says that if Nan marries him he'll give each of us whatever we ask for as a wedding present. I wish I could ask for a ship.'

'Bridegrooms don't give brides' brothers *ships*. It's a cravat pin, usually, or a pair of shoe buckles.'

'Will Verney got a new belt buckle when his sister Clarissa got married,' James admitted. 'He was telling us this morning. But Francis—he does things thoroughly. It comes of owning a fleet of trading ships, I suppose, and dealing in hundreds at a time instead of ones.'

'Not hundreds,' Prudence said. 'Thousands.'

'That's what I mean. Francis is different.'

'Francis may be, but Annaple isn't. She likes things to be—well, peaceable. Romantic, yes, but quiet.'

'Francis used to be quiet,' James said thoughtfully. 'But I think he's changing.'

5

St John the Evangelist's Day

On Evangelist's Day, the Bishop blessed the Gospels in the Market Place, and then they were carried in procession round the town. The Kitsons, however, slept late and missed the ceremony. It was ten o'clock before Prudence woke up. She slid out of bed, being careful not to wake Annaple; pulled on her wrapper and her slippers; and made her way softly downstairs.

The hall windows were open, and she could hear the choirboys chanting in Latin as they turned into Lee Street. They were singing the first chapter of St John's Gospel. She opened the door and went out on the bridge to watch. The procession was just passing the house: she saw the great book with its scarlet silk marker and wide decorated margins, and the candles burning in their tall sticks, and the small silver bell which chimed steadily on a single clear note. Her uncles were pacing along behind the choir. She waved to them cheerfully. Behind them came the Bishop, then the Mayor, who never missed anything, then a straggling crowd of children. Prudence watched them pass, and then went down to the kitchen, made up the fire, and hung the kettle on its great iron hook. She was hunting for Annaple's caraway cakes, which were gritty and over-cooked but better than nothing, when there was a ring at the door. She went upstairs again, yawning, and found Francis's third-day presents waiting on the bridge.

* * *

'*Hens!*' Annaple exclaimed.

'French hens.'

'It's very kind of him, of course, very thoughtful, but I really don't think—'

'You said you wanted hens, my dear.' Papa had lit his first pipe of the day, and was in a good humour. 'Now Francis has sent three. Very considerate of him.'

'Do you think I should accept them, Papa?'

'Certainly, certainly. A very simple, domestic gift. Woodcutter-style.'

Annaple eyed him suspiciously, and he sucked in his cheeks and looked bland.

'Original,' Prudence put in hurriedly.

'Romantic too,' Christopher said. 'French hens, specially imported—'

'Well, I suppose it is very kind of him.'

Prudence fingered the string of yellow shells which had come in a packet labelled *Prudence—to make up for missing France.* 'The only thing is,' she said cautiously, 'he's sent one or two other things as well.'

'Like what?'

'Well, a couple of coops—for the hens and the partridges.' Prudence glossed over the arrival of another partridge, another pear tree, and two more turtle doves. 'A couple of coops to go in the courtyard, two men to fix them up, some nesting boxes, a farmer's boy with a bale of straw, a sack of corn, and some ground-up seashells.'

* * *

It took a considerable time to get the presents carried into the courtyard, the coops and runs set up, the hens and partridges installed, the fowls and the men and the farmer's boy all fed. Annaple told the boy to put the sack of corn and bag of shell in the pantry, but Christopher shifted them to the woodshed—'Otherwise we'll be finding handfuls of shell in Nan's stews.' Prudence took advantage of all the coming and going, the clucks, the suggestions and arguments and hammering, to hang the second cageful of doves in the bedroom window and slip the third partridge into the coop with its fellows and set the third pear tree at the head of the stairs. It was some time before Annaple noticed these additions.

'Those doves—why did you move them up to the bedroom, Pru?'

'I didn't. Not exactly. It's another pair.'

'*Another* pair?' Papa said. 'But this is ridiculous!'

Annaple was thinking. 'That tree at the stairhead—do you mean Francis sent another pear tree as well?'

'With another partridge in it. Yes.'

Papa said to Annaple, 'The thank you letter you sent round yesterday must have been too glowing, my dear.'

'But it was just a polite note, Papa. I said thank you, and how pretty the doves were, and Polly would be glad to have a mate, and how kind it was of him.'

'Well, today I should restrict yourself to simple thanks.'

'But I've already sent today's.'

'Glowing?'

'Warm, at least.' Annaple bit her lips. 'Oh dear.'

'Let us hope that tomorrow he doesn't send another partridge, another pear tree, two more turtle doves, and three more French hens, or this house will be turned into a Noah's Ark.'

'An elephant!' Christopher said happily. 'Wouldn't you like an elephant, Nan?'

'No, I would not.' Annaple was flustered. 'Stop talking nonsense, go and wash your hands—and you'd better begin your own thank you letters—Evangelist's Day already, and not one done. At least a page and a half each, nicely written, mind you say what the present *was*—there's a list in my workbox. If you can't spell something, ask Papa—'

'I can spell something.' James was cheerfully picking bits of straw out of his hair. 'S-o-m-e-t-h-i-n-g.'

'*Not* very amusing,' Annaple said sharply. 'If you

haven't written four letters by tonight, you won't get any supper.'

'What *is* for supper?' Christopher asked cautiously, because sometimes it was an advantage to go without.

'Omelettes. Made with French eggs.'

* * *

But the French hens weren't laying. They crouched in the coop, their feathers indignantly ruffled, and wouldn't eat or drink. Annaple became worried.

'We can't let them starve, poor things.'

'You've been starving *us* for years, Nan.'

'Don't be ridiculous.' She sat on her heels, holding out a handful of corn, and said 'Chuck chuck chuckitty' in a hopeful way. The hens glowered at her.

'Try it in French,' James said.

'I can't see that chuck chuckitty is English precisely. However. Oh dear, they are such silly birds.' She took a hen by its feather scruff and dipped its beak into her hand. It squawked wildly, flapped its wings, and pecked her. 'What is the French for hen, anyway?'

'*Deenay* is French for dinner,' Christopher said.

Annaple called, 'Deenay, deenay, deenay, deenay, deenay, deenay,' over and over, but without success. When at last she gave up, the sky was growing dark and the lantern was alight in the church tower. 'Silly things,' she said crossly, flapping her apron at the sulky French hens. 'I'd rather have English birds any day.'

6

Holy Innocents' Day

On the morning of Holy Innocents' Day, James and Prudence and Christopher went down to the church with all the other town children to watch the choosing of the Boy Bishop. The choirboys lined up in the Market Place around a manger full of straw, stuck with Christmas roses and ivy trails and sprigs of holly. The Bishop sat in his chair in the church porch, with all the local clergy, including the five uncles, clustered around him.

Nine o'clock began to chime. The choirboys went up in turn to pull straws from the manger, and then the choirmaster went round comparing and measuring. He stepped back, bowed to the Bishop, and announced that Will Verney had pulled the shortest straw. The crowd clapped, the choir cheered, and Will flushed and stared hard at the cobbles.

The Bishop stepped down from his chair. He bowed to Will, who ducked his head, and withdrew in good order with the clergy. The choirmaster led Will to the chair, installed him, bowed briefly as if it hurt, looked round, sniffed, and went into the church. The door banged behind him. The crowd burst forward, shouting and cheering, crowned Will with holly, garlanded him with ivy and ribbons, and hoisted him shoulder-high. They processed around the Market Place, laughing and clapping, threatening the stallholders with branches of holly and being paid off with sweetmeats and pennies, and roaring out in chorus the carol of the day:

> 'Lully, lulla, thou little tiny child;
> By by, lully lullay.
> Herod, the king,
> In his raging,
> Chargèd he hath this day
> His men of might,
> In his own sight,
> All young children to slay.
> Lully lulla, thou little tiny child;
> By by, lully lullay.'

The procession turned into Ship Street. The choir-boys ran ahead, banging on the doors of all the houses where there were young children and shouting, 'Ransom your brats, ransom your brats, a penny a piece for your babies.' The pennies showered from the windows. Will dipped his hand into his sack and threw handfuls of nuts and little bags of sugar plums to each ransomed child, and the choirboys stuck sprigs of holly through each door knocker to mark the fact that the price had been paid. The crowd whistled and cheered. At the top of Ship Street they swung left along Keel Alley, Bishop Will rocking precariously on the shifting shoulders; then left again, down Lee Street.

'There was something to be said for Herod's point of view,' Annaple said crossly as the crowd of children swept past. She was irritable because she kept catching herself listening for the doorbell and wondering if Francis would send anything today—and if so, what? And how many of it?

The children swept through the Market Place again, dodged between the stalls, and burst uphill into Green Street. Prudence, carried along by the flood, ran slap into Francis and was nearly knocked off her feet.

'Whoa,' he said, steadying her. 'Gently.'

'Oh, Francis, I didn't hurt you, did I? What are you doing?'

'Going down to the Market—to look for something for Annaple.'

'Oh, dear.' Prudence paused and then tried to explain tactfully that Annaple might not be pleased to get another present—particularly not if a partridge, a pear tree, two turtle doves, and three more French hens came too. But Francis brushed this aside.

'Annaple says she was delighted,' he pointed out, tapping the pocket in which he carried Annaple's polite, grateful thank you notes.

Prudence hesitated. It was impossible not to be pleased by the thought of Annaple trapped in her own good manners. ('But *why* must I say a bag of soapballs is just what I wanted?' Christopher had protested the evening before, when Annaple had driven him to begin his thank you letters. 'If I do, Aunt Rachel will send me another bag *next* year.') But she had another go. 'Papa isn't very pleased, Francis. I did try to explain to him, about how we thought Annaple might be impressed if you sent very imaginative presents, but he only grunted and said it was a pity you had to be imaginative at his expense, although he wished you all success in the enterprise.'

'Oh.' Francis thought this over. 'Perhaps he'd like a present too.'

'No, no,' Prudence said quickly. 'Papa isn't a bit romantic.'

'Not romantic presents like Annaple's. Something ordinary. Some of the wine we got when we went to France. Would he like that? Say six bottles a day.'

Taken aback, Prudence thought this over and admitted that Papa would probably like it very much. 'If you say six bottles a day, he won't mind if you send Annaple an—an elephant.'

'Would she like an elephant? Because I expect it could be arranged, though it would take rather a long time—'

'No, no, *indeed* not,' Prudence said urgently.

'Well, then, what would she like?'

'Birds.' It was the first thing that came into

Prudence's head. 'English birds. So she said yesterday. But, Francis, I really don't think—'

But when she saw the cages of songbirds in the market, she forgot all about what she didn't think. Thrushes and robins, finches and larks, they sat on their bare perches, trapped in wickerwork bells, draggled and cold and silent. There were three dozen for sale, and urged on by Prudence, Francis bought them all. Prudence and he struggled back up Green Street with cages dangling from every finger and strings of cages looped around their necks.

When they reached Francis's house, they couldn't get in because Francis didn't have a spare hand with which to open the door. He pulled the bell rope with his teeth, making Prudence giggle, and his housekeeper appeared. 'Mr Vere!' she said, staring. 'What in the world have you bought now?'

'Just a few birds, Mrs Bowen.'

The housekeeper sighed, but led the way upstairs to the parlour, which was on a decidedly Francis scale. It had been made by knocking two rooms into one, so that it had four doors, six windows, and two fireplaces. Two great log fires were blazing on the hearths. The room was warm and fresh, smelling of wax and applewood.

The housekeeper brought wine and cheese cakes for Francis, milk and gingerbread for Prudence, and after a resigned look at the birds, fresh water and seed for them. Prudence tasted her gingerbread, which was delicious, and made a brave effort to persuade Francis to let his present-giving tail gently away. But it was clear that she was making no impression, so in the end she gave up and sat peaceably watching the fire and eating her gingerbread while Francis told her how pretty and charming Annaple was.

A robin began to chirp tentatively, and presently the other birds responded, first with thin doubtful calls and then, growing bolder, with long triumphant whistles and trills. When for an instant Prudence closed her eyes, she imagined herself back in the greenwood at midsummer.

* * *

'You can set them free!' Prudence said impatiently.

'The birds, yes. But what am I supposed to do with those wretched hens? Not to mention another partridge,' Annaple said crossly, mentioning not just the partridge but everything else as well. 'Another pear tree? Another pair of turtle doves? And probably another hen coop too. This is ridiculous.'

'I knew you were making those thank you letters too enthusiastic, my dear,' Papa said; but he said it absent-mindedly, stroking the bottles of fine French wine. His own thank you letter, dashed off a few minutes before, had been very enthusiastic indeed.

'I shall write and tell him to stop.'

'He mayn't listen,' James said. 'He's enjoying himself. And once he gets an idea into his head—'

'What he gets in, he can get out.'

'It would be much simpler to marry him,' Christopher said hopefully.

'You don't know what you're talking about.'

'You *wanted* him to be romantic, and now he is. I don't know why you're so cross—'

'I am not cross.' Annaple looked at the chirping birds, and her face changed. 'Poor little things, at least we can let them fly.'

She opened the door of the cage. The four birds hopped to the doorway, poked their heads out, and decided to stay where they were. It took half an hour's persuasion and crumb-scattering before two of them cautiously spread their wings, flew up into the air, circled, and settled on the window sill; there they stayed. Christopher opened the window, Annaple flapped her apron, and the birds flew hastily back into the cage.

'They know when they're well off,' Papa said; but so did he, and after another look at the wine, he shut the window and went off to nail up the third cageful of turtle doves and to install the partridge and the hens in the courtyard.

Christopher insisted on practising his trumpet that evening. 'If you don't stop that dreadful noise,' Annaple said, 'I shall take that trumpet away and burn it.'

'I shouldn't think you could, my dear,' Papa said mildly. 'One needs a very hot fire to melt metal.'

'Then I'll drop it down the well.'

'Oh no, you won't,' Christopher said indignantly. 'I have to practise, don't I? And it's cold in the attic.'

'You don't have to practise here and now.'

'I always thought you fancied yourself as that girl in the nursery rhyme, that silly creature who had music wherever she went? So romantic, you used to say; why, there was even that day you sewed bells on your petticoat to see what it would be like—'

'And Papa said, had someone let a flock of sheep loose in the street, or was it a stray cat that had got in,' James remembered, grinning.

'Very amusing,' Annaple said tartly. 'Just because I happened to make some odd remark about a nursery

56

rhyme. And in any case, you couldn't call that squawking, music.'

'It's at least as much music as the wails you get out of
that wretched harp,' Christopher retorted.

He blew a loud and tuneless note and Annaple
snatched the trumpet away. 'I simply cannot stand it a
moment longer—my head is aching—the noise goes
right through me—'

Papa took the trumpet and put it in his coat pocket.
Christopher looked thoughtfully at Annaple. 'You'll be
sorry,' he said.

7

St Thomas of Canterbury's Day

Next morning when the doorbell rang the Kitsons were having breakfast in the parlour. Annaple flushed and went on stirring sugar into her porridge—'If you marry Francis,' Christopher said, 'you needn't ever lift a spoon again'—Papa looked at the ceiling, and Prudence and James and Christopher ran for the stairs. Annaple began, 'Don't be so inquisitive—' but they were already out of earshot.

There was a crowd in the street. A man with a cage of songbirds. A man with a cage of turtle doves. A man with three furious French hens. A man with a partridge clucking anxiously in a pear tree. A man with six bottles of wine. Two workmen with tools and wood. A farmer's boy with a sack of corn. A crowd of children. Several women who were on their way to market and had stopped to see the fun. 'Whatever is it, then? Is it true what they're saying, that Francis Vere's trying to persuade her, but she won't have him?' (Annaple, watching from the parlour window, drew back quickly when she

saw the women.) And last of all, a boy with a large wicker basket.

'Oh, do you think it's a puppy?' Prudence asked eagerly.

'Five puppies, you mean. Papa won't take kindly to it, if so.'

The workmen and the messengers knew their way about by now.

'Don't you worry about us,' the first man said cheerfully, leading the way down the kitchen stairs. 'We know what's where.'

'Oh, is it a puppy?' Prudence demanded, as the

messenger boy put the wicker basket down on the stairs. The boy grinned but shook his head.

Christopher said sadly, 'I was hoping it would be a horse. Like in the nursery rhyme, you know. *Ride a cock horse to Banbury Cross—rings on her fingers, bells on her toes, she shall have music wherever she goes.* A white horse—or even better, *five* white horses. One each—'

'Papa would never agree to our keeping a horse.'

'No, I suppose that's what Francis thought.'

James and Christopher struggled upstairs with the basket and dumped it on the table. Annaple looked at it doubtfully.

'What is it?'

'We don't know, but we're longing to. Do open it, Nan.'

Annaple, pretending to be unconcerned, hummed to herself as she unstrapped the basket and lifted the lid. Prudence craned to see.

'What is it, Nan? What is it?'

'I don't know—' Cautiously, at arms' length, Annaple folded back layers of wrapping paper. 'Christopher!' She swung round to blaze at her brother. 'You told him! Oh, how could you—'

'Told who what? What's Kit done?'

'Told Francis about last night. That wretched nursery rhyme—' Annaple lifted out a great loop of ribbon strung with bells. 'There are strings and strings and strings of bells—' She raised her voice above the tinkling. 'It's too bad of you, Christopher. Papa, speak to him—'

But Papa was amused. 'Bells, my dear? Well, at least they take no feeding or watering. And how very suitable for St Thomas's Day.'

'Now you can have bells on your toes, Nan, and bells in your ears, and bells round your neck, and bells on your petticoat—'

'I shall never forgive you.' The bells tinkled endlessly. She lifted out the last tangle of ribbon. There were more presents underneath. 'Really, Francis is too foolish—' She picked up two flower pots with seedlings in them. '*Canterbury bells,*' she read from the label. '*Keep well watered. Plant out in March.* Plant out where? Francis knows perfectly well we don't have a garden.'

'He's probably planning to send round half a dozen window boxes.'

'If he does, I shall use them for firewood.'

'You're setting us a very bad example, Nan—you should be grateful to Francis. After all, you told Kit he ought to be grateful for those soapballs Aunt Rachel sent him.'

Annaple picked some miniature horses out of the basket and balanced them on the back of her hand. 'Quite ridiculous,' she said helplessly.

At the bottom of the basket were a dozen lavender bags, two sacks of Banbury buns, and a small red leather pouch.

'Go on, Nan, undo it. Or are you scared?'

Annaple gave Christopher a furious look. She untied

the thong, stood well back, and tipped out the contents. Five gold rings rolled across the table. Annaple stared at them.

'But I can't possibly accept those, I shall have to send them back at once, they're much too expensive.'

'Not for Francis. He has masses of money.'

'Don't talk about money, it isn't polite.'

'But that's exactly what *you're* doing, Nan.'

Annaple flushed. 'Papa, what should I do?'

'Whatever you think proper, my dear. Of course, if you insist on returning the rings, Francis might be very hurt. And while *one* gold ring might appear—well, significant, five simply appear—let us say, generous.'

Christopher began to say something about all the uncles wanting to do the marrying, so that five gold rings would be needed instead of one, and James kicked him hard on the ankle.

Annaple said, 'I simply do not know what I should do.'

'Well, that makes a nice change,' Christopher muttered.

* * *

On St Thomas's Day the Bishop held a Blessing of Keys, so Annaple collected the keys from every door and drawer and coffer and cupboard in the house and sent Prudence down to the church with them; she scattered great handfuls of crumbs and bacon rind for St Thomas's sparrows, since these were the kind of traditions she approved of; and when the bell-ringers began to ring Canterbury Triples in the church tower, she opened the window so that she could hear better. But the rush of cold air made Francis's bells, which James had strung round the parlour, swing and tinkle, and she shut the window again hastily, and presently, as the ding-ding-ding went on steadily from the tower, she pressed her hands to her ears and said, 'My head aches with all this clanging.'

'Usually you say how romantic it is.'

'Usually I'm not being plagued by a madman. Papa, couldn't you make him stop?'

'My dear, all you have to do is to write and ask him nicely.'

'But he doesn't believe me.' She sighed. She looked at the turtle doves in the window and the robins on the sill and the loops of bells dangling from the ceiling and the rings scattered on the table. She thought of the pear trees and the buns and the miniature horses and all the livestock in the courtyard.

'Oh dear,' she said. 'I wish I were a goosegirl with no problems. Just wandering through the fields, barefoot in the dew. A little red shawl over my head. A line of geese. And,' she added crossly, thinking of the sulky French hens, 'plenty of eggs.'

* * *

Christopher opened the door and slipped on to the bridge. Francis was waiting, wrapped in a big dark cloak, with a hat pulled down on his forehead.

'What on earth are you disguised as?' Christopher asked, puzzled.

'Something official, I thought. A lamplighter, perhaps. Or a stream inspector.' He peered thoughtfully down at the water. 'It looks very clean.'

'It should, Annaple makes us scrub out our bit of gutter once a week. You look more like a spy than a Mayor's Man.'

'Well, so I am. Hurry, or Nan will look out of the window and see us. What sort of things has she said today?'

8

Churching Day

On the morning of Churching Day the people going down to market and the people coming back with their purchases collected in little groups in Lee Street, making polite conversation about the weather and the children and how to use up leftover Christmas beef, and all waiting to see if the stories about Francis Vere and Annaple Kitson were true. Annaple flounced down to the kitchen as soon as she was dressed. She refused to take any responsibility for the livestock; James, Prudence, and Christopher had to do all the feeding and cleaning out. While Annaple stayed in the kitchen, crossly snipping bacon rind and pretending she wasn't a bit interested in possible presents, the children toiled around the house and the courtyard, feeding the partridges, the doves, the hens, and the birds, watering the pear trees, and cleaning out the coops.

'At least gold rings are no trouble,' James said, when at last they gathered in the parlour for breakfast. 'They don't even need polishing.'

'And they take up very little room,' Papa added. 'I trust whatever comes today will be small and simple. A bunch of ribbons, perhaps.'

'But, Papa, Francis is trying to be romantic—'

'Half a dozen pomegranates, then. Or some periwinkle plants. Ah, Annaple my dear. Good morning.'

Annaple put her tray down on the table. 'Only bacon,' she said. 'Those tiresome hens still aren't laying.'

'Why have you got your old blue dress on, Nan? It's Churching Day.'

'I'm not going this year.'

'But, Nan—'

'I won't have people gossiping about me—pointing fingers—whispering together—*That's her, that's the girl whose lover sent her five gold rings, four calling birds*—'

'*Three* French hens—' James chanted.

'*Two* turtle doves—'

'And a partridge in a pear tree!' Christopher shouted cheerfully.

'All very silly!' snapped Annaple, and went off to the kitchen where she meant to stay until the procession of presents was safely over.

'The bacon tastes odd today,' Papa said, poking doubtfully at the rashers, which Annaple had mistakenly fried in candle grease instead of pork dripping. He cut snippets off the rashers and fed them to the songbirds, who hopped and chirruped blithely round his plate.

Prudence opened the window, which set the bells jangling, and James, Christopher, and she leant out to wave to their friends and call, 'Hello—' and 'How are you—?' and 'Are you having a merry Christmas?' The crowd was considerably more numerous by this time.

As nine o'clock chimed from the church tower, they heard small boys shouting at the end of the street. The procession of messengers came into sight.

'What is it, James? Can you see? Quick, what is it?'

James gave a shout of delight. 'Geese! By the Lord Harry, *geese*!'

'We'd better rush down and open the door before Nan can bolt it.'

They took the stairs three at a time, flung the door open, and ran out on to the bridge. The procession wound its way up the street through the holiday crowd. First six goosegirls, in brown skirts and red scarves, each carrying a big white goose. The geese were all cackling and shooting out their long necks. After the girls, the usual messengers with cages of doves and birds, and angry hens held upside down, and a placid partridge tucked up in her pear tree; a boy with a bag of rings; a boy with a straw nest in which lay a dozen big brown eggs; a dressmaker's apprentice carrying a deeply-fringed red shawl, several yards of brown material, and a white apron; a gang of plumbers with pipes and spanners; a gang of builders with trowels and bags of lime; a boy pushing a wheelbarrow full of pieces of stone; the local gravedigger pushing a second barrow, this one full of topsoil and slabs of turf; and last of all, three errand boys with wine for Papa, bunches of Christmas roses for

Annaple and Prudence, sugar plums for James and Christopher, and stone bottles of beer and bundles of bread, cheese, and beef for the workmen.

'I must say,' James said, 'Francis thinks of everything! He must be enjoying himself enormously.'

'Francis thinks of a great deal too much!' Annaple had come flouncing up the kitchen stairs. To the goosegirls she said, 'I am sorry, but you must take those geese away.'

'But we can't, miss.'

'There simply isn't room for them here.'

'But we won't get our money unless we deliver them *here*, miss. And we can't leave them in the street, the Mayor'll be on to us.'

Annaple looked from their faces, pinched with worry at the idea of losing their money, to their feet, which were bare and cold, and she said helplessly, 'Oh, very well.'

'*Not* so romantic,' James whispered to Prudence. 'Francis is being rather clever.'

The goosegirls filed across the bridge. 'They're all a-laying, miss,' the first one said consolingly to Annaple.

Annaple, who was looking dazed, let the other messengers in without a word, but woke up sharply at the appearance of the plumbers.

'No, no—we have a perfectly good well, and the drains were checked only last year.'

'Now, don't get flustered,' the first plumber said. 'It's for the geese, you see. So's they'll have somewhere to splash about. Don't pay any heed to us, we know what we're about, and we won't make no mess.'

'But what's that?' Annaple asked in horror as the first wheelbarrow trundled over the bridge.

'It's a bit of a pond, that's all. With a decorative kerb.'

'So I see,' Annaple said limply, staring at a marble river god who was surging up out of the protective folds of sacking.

'And the gravedigger's here to lay a grass verge round the edge.'

The gravedigger pushed his barrowload past Annaple. Behind him came the master carpenter. 'Mr Johnson—what on earth are you doing here?'

'I've come to measure the windows, Anne love.'

'The *windows*?'

'For window boxes. And young Francis is sending round a load of kindling as well, because you mentioned you might be needing some. And would you care for a few water lilies for your bit of stream, to brighten it up, and what flowers would you fancy for the window boxes?'

Annaple pressed her hands to her head. 'This is impossible. Pru, where's Papa?'

'Still in the parlour.'

Annaple ran upstairs. 'Papa, you have to stop this, it's getting completely out of hand.'

'Just a few house improvements, my dear, or so James tells me. And geese are very good watchmen, you know. The ancient Greeks used to keep flocks to guard their buildings.'

'They'll warn off all the thieves, Nan,' James said, grinning.

'I don't care what the ancient Greeks may or may not have done. And I doubt if we have anything worth stealing.'

'There are your gold rings.'

'If I thought those wretched rings would draw thieves to the house, I should throw them into the sea. Now I shan't sleep a wink for worrying.'

'Don't be ridiculous, my dear, there isn't the slightest risk.'

'Let's go down and help the men,' Christopher said.

Annaple said, 'I am going upstairs, and there I shall stay until the house is our own again.'

'Are you going to write your thank you letters, Nan? Because if so, remember to put in what the presents *were*. Six geese, five gold rings, four calling birds, three French hens, two turtle doves, and a partridge in a pear tree—'

'Kit, be quiet.'

'—and if there's anything you can't spell, just ask Papa. A page and a half at least, mind.'

* * *

Annaple went off in a huff and shut herself into the bedroom, where she stayed while the plumbers and the builders got on with the conversion of the courtyard, and the workmen fixed up a new coop, and the grave-digger laid his turf and spread netting over it.

James was writing down measurements for the carpenter, Christopher was helping the builders to slap clay and lime around, and Prudence was in the hall, arranging the pear trees on the staircase. 'Be careful, Jem,' she said, as James, clutching rule, pencil, and paper, squeezed past on his way to measure the parlour window. 'Try not to brush against the twigs. Do you think Nan will sulk upstairs all day?'

'The way she flounced up there, yes. She's cross, you know, because really she'd like to join in the fun, only she's too much on her dignity.'

'Oh dear.'

'No dinner, d'you think? Well, no loss really.'

'It's a good thing those geese are laying. There's hardly anything left to eat in the house, except for those sugar plums.'

Annaple wouldn't go down to the church that evening.

'But, Nan, you always say it's one of your favourite Christmas things.'

'Not this year. I shall stay at home.'

Papa stayed too—'When the wind comes off the sea, a wise man's snug indoors'—and so did Christopher—'All those screeching babies, how can you bear it?'—but Prudence meant to go, and James said he would go with her. 'I can't bear the babies either, but I like the Churching carol.'

Annaple checked them over before they left. She didn't mean to nag, but Francis's courtship, and the way everyone else was enjoying it at her expense, had got badly on her nerves, and she had to take it out on some-body. 'Have you found a clean handkerchief, James? Your hair's untidy. Where are your gloves, Pru?'

'I don't know,' Prudence said. 'They've disappeared.'

'Gloves can't get up and walk. Where did you leave them? No, never mind, you'll be late—you'd better borrow mine.'

'It isn't all that cold out—'

'No, but it's church, after all, you ought to wear gloves.'

Prudence sighed, James grinned; and Annaple said, 'And if you see Francis—'

'Yes?' James prompted; but Annaple had changed her mind. 'Nothing,' she said. 'You won't see him, anyway. He never goes to the Churching ceremonies.'

'Suppose this year he does?'

Annaple hesitated. Then she said, 'If he does—if he does, don't you dare say anything that might encourage him.'

'But he doesn't need encouragement now,' James pointed out. 'He might have done at the beginning, but now he's sliding down the slipway under his own power.'

'And who gave him the first push, I'd like to know?' Annaple retorted.

'You did, Nan. Are you ready, Pru? Come on, then.'

The church was full of people when they arrived, but they found seats about halfway down the aisle, opposite their Aunt Rachel. The Bishop was already in his place at the altar rail. Francis, arriving late, squashed into the pew beside Prudence.

'Where's Nan? I thought this was one of her favourite Christmas services.'

'Well, yes. But she thought she'd stay home this year.'

'She's sulking,' James said cheerfully.

'Did she like the geese?'

Prudence hedged. 'She's a bit irritable at the moment—' Francis, however, didn't seem worried.

'Wait till she sees tomorrow's,' he said happily.

'What *is* tomorrow's?'

'A surprise. Shush—here they come.'

A baby whimpered in the stillness. Mary and Joseph came slowly down the aisle. Joseph was carrying two turtle doves in a cage. Their crooning sounded softly below the humming as Mary lulled her son.

The Bishop took the baby into his arms and blessed it. An old man, the oldest in the town, sang the *Nunc Dimittis* in a thin, cracked voice. Then the Bishop handed the baby to an old woman, and she rocked it gently and hummed the Churching carol, which was so old that the words had faded into the murmur of the tune.

One by one the women of the town brought their babies, all the babies born since last Christmas, to be blessed and prayed over. Prudence watched them go past. Some of the babies were sleepy, some wide awake and wailing. One or two could totter along on their own feet. She saw Will Verney's newly-married sister Clarissa, who was sitting across the aisle, lean forward to watch one solemn, wobbly small boy. Prudence remembered the Christmas when Mama had carried Christopher to the altar rail, and wondered if she would ever bring her own son, her own daughter, for blessing.

They came out of the church into a calm winter night and watched the doves, freed from their cage, circle overhead. Francis walked up Lee Street with James and Prudence. 'I won't come in,' he said, when they reached the house. A woman passed them, hurrying home because her baby, tightly wrapped in her shawl, was crying fretfully. Prudence looked up and saw a haze of candlelight in the bedroom window and Annaple, all alone, staring down at the street, betrayed by the fiery outlining of her head as the candles shone through her hair.

9

New Year's Eve

On the last day of the year the Mayor's men always processed around the town and the children came running out of the houses for the traditional gifts of oranges and buns. But this year the men found themselves marching up and down empty streets. Their bell clanged sadly, and their calls of 'Come out, come out, the year is dying' had no effect. All the children and most of their parents were in Lee Street, outside the Kitsons' house, waiting for a different procession. The grown-ups weren't even bothering to make polite conversation about the price of candles and the chances of snow: they were openly wondering what Francis would send today. The children were admiring the dolphin-mounted marble boys which the builders had set on either side of the way to the Kitsons' door. Water spouted merrily from the dolphins' mouths into the stream.

'Where on *earth* did those come from!' Annaple

demanded in astonishment, as she looked down from the parlour window.

'They were left over from the pond, and it seemed a pity to waste them. The plumbers fixed up the water pipes.'

Annaple said crossly, 'Look at all those gossips cackling away down there, just like so many geese. Papa, surely you could speak to Francis?'

'He would take more notice of you, my dear.'

'Pru, do shut the window, those tiresome bells are clinking away—James, don't tilt your chair like that—'

Even with the window shut they could still hear the crowd talking and laughing down in the street. The turtle doves murmured, the sparrows chirruped; and Annaple said suddenly, 'I've only tried to keep things up to the mark. Maybe I've been a touch fanciful, but just to add a bit of colour to ordinary life—the mending, the cooking—'

'*Cooking* she calls it.'

'He only tried to be an ordinary lover, my dear. But you wouldn't listen. So now he is being a merry one.'

The church bells began to chime nine o'clock. The noise in the street grew louder. Someone cheered. 'Sit *down*,' Annaple said sharply, as Prudence and James and Christopher pushed back their chairs. 'Stay where you are.'

The doorbell clanged. The children looked at Annaple; Annaple looked at her plate. Papa hummed to himself. *Christmas is coming, the goose is getting fat, please put a penny in the old man's hat*. 'We should have an excellent goose next Christmas,' he said, spooning up his boiled egg. 'Really, these geese lay wonderfully big eggs, this one is a meal in itself.'

'Which is lucky,' Prudence said, 'because the pantry's empty, and Nan says she won't go marketing.'

'All those people staring and whispering,' Annaple said defensively.

'Dear child, you shouldn't let a little friendly interest get on your nerves.'

The bell clanged again. There was a new outburst of cheering down in the street. Annaple sat tight; and Prudence, glancing at her face, frowned at Christopher, who was nearly wild with impatience, and made a brave push at the conversation. 'We'll do the marketing for you, Nan.'

'You won't do any such thing. That's just an excuse to go plotting with Francis.'

The bell clanged for the third time. Papa said mildly, 'Don't you think you should answer it, my dear?'

Annaple folded her napkin and stood up. Papa put his hand on Christopher's knee, to restrain him from jumping up to follow her. She walked to the window. She was as stiff as a wooden doll. But then, as she looked down into the street, she came alive again: astonished, annoyed, disbelieving. 'Oh *Francis*—'

'What is it, Nan?'

'Oh, do tell us.'

'Don't be so mean, Nan,' begged Christopher, wriggling wildly on his chair.

Annaple put her hands to her mouth. 'I should never, *never* have told him how much I loved that fairytale.'

'I do feel, my dear child, that you must have been exceedingly rash in some of your remarks to Francis.'

'*Which* fairytale?' Christopher was jumping up and down.

'The one where the seven princes were turned into swans—their sister had to weave nettle shirts—'

'Swans!'

Prudence and James and Christopher ran to the window just as the bell rang again. 'Oh, how lovely!' Prudence said.

Seven swans were bobbing on the stream. The water from the dolphins' mouths showered over them. The leading swan reached up, seized the bell-pull in its beak, and tugged. The bell rang again and the crowd clapped and cheered. Prudence said, 'Oh, aren't they clever?'

James turned to look at Annaple. 'What other fairytales did you tell Francis you liked, Nan? Are we going to wake up tomorrow to find a pumpkin—'

'Eight pumpkins,' Christopher put in cheerfully.

'—*eight* pumpkins on the doorstep?'

'Do be quiet, both of you—'

'Look!' Christopher called. 'Here come the messengers.'

Six more goosegirls with six more geese. A boy with a bag of rings. A string of messengers carrying birdcages.

A man with a partridge in a pear tree. The carpenter
with a stack of window boxes. A boy with a barrow full
of earth. Another boy carrying seed boxes, a trowel, and
a large watering pot. A cartload of kindling wood. A boy
with a bulging sack. A boy with a parcel tied up in brown
paper.

Prudence, James, and Christopher ran down to open
the door. The messengers clumped downstairs to the
kitchen and the courtyard, and the carpenter, whistling
cheerfully, got to work fixing up his window boxes in the
hall windows. This left the children with the bag of
rings, the sack, and the brown paper parcel. They carried these things off to the parlour, where Annaple said

they could open them if they chose; she wasn't interested. But she watched covertly, just the same.

James ripped the parcel open and began to laugh. It was a loom: a small stout affair complete with shuttle. After this, they weren't surprised to find the sack was full of nettles—'Careful, you'll sting yourself—*dear* Francis—look, there's a note as well—'

'Saying what?' James asked hopefully.

Prudence began to giggle. '*I am credibly informed that if cooked slowly over a close fire, nettles make a nourishing broth, and can indeed be served in place of cabbages and similar greenstuff.*'

Fortunately, since Annaple was extremely annoyed, they were interrupted by the clang of the bell. The swans were getting hungry and were impatient for breakfast. The children ran to the window and saw that the Mayor's men had arrived, with their sackfuls of buns and oranges, and were distributing gifts to the crowd. The choirboys pulled their buns to pieces and fed them to the swans. An enterprising child balanced oranges on the waterspouts. The bright round fruit bobbed merrily up and down.

'Swans!' Annaple said helplessly, as Christopher threw crusts from the window.

'Highly romantic birds, I believe.'

'Oh, Papa, please. Swans—*seven* swans.'

'*And* six geese,' Christopher said happily.

'*And* five gold rings—'

'*And* four calling birds—'

'*Four calling birds*,' Will Verney sang cheerfully down in the street.

'*Three* French hens,' James chanted.

'*Three French hens*,' the crowd echoed, picking up the idea.

Christopher leant out to conduct them with his egg spoon.

'Two turtle doves—'

'*Two turtle doves—*'

'And a partridge in a pear tree—'

'*And a par—art—ri—idge in a pear tree*,' they all sang together.

Annaple shut the window.

* * *

That night the Kitsons sat up to watch the New Year in. The carol singers came tramping round again, with lanterns and wreaths of holly. Prudence drew back the parlour curtains and opened the window a crack. The Christmas candle flame dipped in the cold air and the loops of bells clinked together.

> 'Here we come a-wassailing
> Among the leaves so green,
> Here we come a-wandering,
> So fair to be seen:
> Love and joy come to you,
> And to you your wassail too,

And God bless you, and send you
A happy New Year.'

The voices were fresh and clear. 'Rather charming in
their way,' Papa said, filling his pipe. 'Less arranged
than the choir.' He glanced at Annaple and added,
'Romantic.'

'Papa, please. Don't breathe on the windows like that,
Kit.'

'You're so cross these days, Nan.'

'Good Master and good Mistress,
While you're sitting by the fire
Pray think of us poor children
Who are wandering in the mire—'

Annaple sighed and fetched her purse. She took out a
handful of pennies, and when the singers had sung
through seven verses and seven refrains, she let
Prudence and James and Christopher throw money into
the leather buckets. Most of Prudence's pennies went
into the stream. The swans had withdrawn, hissing,
under the bridge, but their angry heads snaked out each
time a penny splashed into the water.

The wassailers lined up, at a safe distance from the
swans, to sing their goodbye. Christopher tried to
accompany them on his trumpet, but Annaple took it
away and plugged it with a wine cork. The voices came
merrily up from the street.

'God bless Ralph Kitson of this house,
Likewise Annaple too,
Prudence and James and Christopher
That round the table go:
And all your kin and kinsfolk,
That dwell both far and near;
We wish you a merry Christmas,
And a happy New Year.'

The singers crossed the street and began all over again. Prudence shut the window. Annaple trimmed the wick of the great candle and the flame burned up freshly. Over half the candle had burned away; half of Christmas gone.

Just before twelve they gathered again by the window. Prudence and James blew out all the candles except the great Christmas one. The five of them held hands. All over town the candles were going out. At a minute to twelve the yellow glow of the lantern in the church tower glimmered and disappeared.

In silence they watched and waited. Then, as the great bell chimed the first stroke of twelve, the lantern-light sprang out again. Annaple lit a taper from the Christmas candle, shielding the flame with her fingers, and held it to the branches of fresh candles that stood round the room. New candle flames pricked the darkness outside. As the last stroke of twelve chimed out, bells began to ring all over town. Boys came marching down the street, with drums and whistles and fifes and fiddles playing merrily, and lanterns swinging on sticks to light their way. The swans, a white glimmer of feathers under the bridge, hissed angrily. The geese and the hens cackled crossly in the courtyard. The songbirds and the doves woke up, decided it must be dawn, and began to sing.

'A merry New Year, children,' said Papa.

10

New Year's Day

As soon as breakfast was over on New Year's morning, Prudence and James and Christopher gathered by the window. Annaple was sitting at the table, pretending she didn't care, but when Christopher shouted, 'Look—here they come!' she got up and strolled over to join the children.

Seven more swans came sailing up the gutter, the usual procession of workmen and messengers made its way through the usual crowd, but Prudence hardly noticed them. She was staring at eight dairymaids, with yokes across their shoulders and milking stools under their arms, leading eight small cows garlanded with ivy.

'I will not have those cows in here!' Annaple said furiously. 'A swannery at the front door, a courtyard full of geese and hens and partridges, every window blocked with birdcages, an orchard on the stairs—I can put up with these things if I must—if Papa won't do anything to stop this silliness—but I will *not* have this house turned into a cowshed.'

James said quickly, 'I'll go down and explain.'

'So will I.'

'And me.'

As they squeezed downstairs between the pear trees they could hear the crowd beginning merrily, '*On the* EIGHTH *day of Christmas my true love sent to me,* EIGHT *maids a-milking—*'

Prudence opened the door. 'Oh dear,' she said, 'please—I'm sorry—we're very grateful—but we simply can't let those cows in, there just isn't room—'

'That's all right, miss,' the first maid said. 'Mr Vere's hired a fine cowshed for us, outside the town walls. It's only the milk we've to leave.'

'How much milk does one get from eight cows?' James asked hopefully.

'About twelve buckets. They're fine milkers.'

'Twelve buckets! But one bucket usually lasts us for two clear days.'

'And Mr Vere's sent a butter churn,' the milkmaid said, 'because some remark the young lady once made led him to think she might have a fancy to make her own butter. And some butter pats, and a copper pan for scalding cream, and muslin bags for making cream cheese.'

'Oh, Francis is wonderful!'

The cows formed a circle. The maids set down their stools, unhooked their buckets, and began milking. The crowd stood round, admiring, and the messengers began to troop across the bridge.

'A bag of gold rings for Miss Kitson.'

'On the table, please.'

'Wine and tobacco for Mr Kitson.'

'Upstairs, please, in the parlour. Mind the trees—Oh dear, *more* hens.'

'Very special hens. From France.'

'I know, I know.'

'Six geese, miss.'

'Two turtle doves, miss.'

'Four thrushes, miss.'

'One partridge. One pear tree.'

'One set of cream jugs.'

Christopher was counting on his fingers. 'That makes—that makes fourteen turtle doves—eighteen hens—twenty calling birds—twenty gold rings—eighteen geese—fourteen swans—and eight partridges in eight pear trees.'

'And assorted dairy equipment,' James said, as a man staggered by with a butter churn.

'And all that milk.'

'What can one make with milk?'

'Junket—custard—syllabub—'

'Another sack of corn for the geese,' Christopher said.

'A dozen water lilies for the ponds.'

'Bulbs for the parlour window boxes, herbs for the kitchen ones, primroses for the bedrooms—'

'*And* a special breakfast for the swans,' Prudence said, as two bakers' boys dumped baskets of stale cake by the gutter.

'Letter to Miss Kitson from the Mayor,' the last messenger said. 'Sign here, please.'

* * *

The Mayor's letter annoyed Annaple very much. It told her that if she had any idea of selling dairy produce, she should bear in mind that a licence was required. '*Applications for licences,*' the Mayor wrote, '*cannot be considered until after the Feast of the Three Kings at the close of the Christmas holiday.*'

'Very well,' Annaple said, 'I shall give it away.'

But apparently she wasn't allowed to do that either. 'Only to the Orphanage and the Vere Almshouses,' Papa said. 'Otherwise you'll be putting the dairies out of business. It's the balance of trade, my dear.'

Annaple sighed. She went across to the window to draw the curtains and in a sudden burst of annoyance, jerked them too hard. The curtains ripped away from their rings, the rod jumped out of its socket, and everything came down on Annaple's head.

'Oh, holy Maria—' Annaple exclaimed, in pure exasperation, 'Pru, come and help me—Kit, pick up those wretched rings—'

It took several minutes to tidy up the mess. Annaple, flushed and untidy, sat down to sew the rings back on the curtain. 'The thread had rotted right through,' she said, examining the tattered ends.

'They're twenty years old, those curtains,' Papa said, thinking back. 'I brought Elizabeth—your mother—I brought her home to this house on the evening of our wedding day, and she hung those curtains up straightaway. She sat there, sewing the rings on to them, while I nailed up the rods—they were a wedding present from her sister Rachel, and she wanted Rachel to see them already hanging at our windows when she passed our house on her way to school next morning—'

Annaple bit her lip and bent her head over the sewing. James banged in the last nail and jumped down to join Prudence and Christopher, who were taking turns at the churning.

'The milk's still sloshing around in there,' Christopher said, despairingly, rubbing his tired wrists. 'I don't believe it will ever turn into butter. Whatever did you say to Francis, Nan, to make him think you fancied playing dairymaid?'

'Nothing. At least,' Annaple said defensively, 'I might have made a casual remark at some time, but—'

'There you are, you see.'

'What other casual remarks have you made, Nan?'

Annaple flushed and said she didn't remember; and when Christopher and James and Prudence began to argue happily about what Francis might send next day— '*Nine* of whatever it is, don't forget'—she cut across them tartly. 'Stop gossiping away like the old women in the Market Place. I'm six rings short, they must have rolled through that crack in the floorboards. I do wish you would have it mended, Papa.'

'Dear child, whenever I turn round in this house I see a carpenter or some other kind of handyman—'

'Use your gold rings, Nan,' James suggested. 'You've got more than enough. We'll be the only house in town with a fortune on the curtain rods.'

'You're as vulgar a show-off as Francis Vere,' Annaple said crossly, and pricked herself on her needle.

11

Dancing Day

The French hens woke up early and began squawking their hatred of England. The geese and the swans uncurled themselves and hissed. The partridges began to cluck. The songbirds chirruped and fluted. Soon after this the Kitsons stirred and yawned, pulled pillows and blankets over their heads, and finally gave it up, opened their eyes, and stretched.

'This isn't my idea of the dawn chorus,' Annaple said crossly, as she sat up in bed and unplaited her hair.

'Not romantic enough?' Prudence said. 'Would you rather have a piper? Oh, how lovely, it's Dancing Day. I must find my red shoes.'

The crowd began gathering soon after eight o'clock. Christopher took out jugs of milk for them. 'I don't care if the Balance of Trade tips right over,' Annaple said as she poached the breakfast eggs in milk.

A little before nine o'clock, Francis came to call. The crowd began to sing. '*On the* FIRST *day of Christmas my true love sent to me—*'

Prudence ran down to let him in. 'She isn't in a very good temper, Francis. I hope whatever you're sending today is easy to take care of?'

'Couldn't be easier,' Francis said cheerfully. 'How are you, Pru? I haven't seen you in town for days.'

'Nan won't go out, she says people are whispering and pointing fingers, and we can't go either because she says we encourage you and give you ideas, and we must just go without the marketing.'

'Never mind, eggs and milk are very good for you,' Francis said. 'But perhaps I could send round a few things for the pantry. It's a pity Nan minds, everybody else is enjoying it. Particularly me.'

'Well, I'm glad of that, because it doesn't seem to have been such a good idea after all. From the point of view of getting Annaple to marry you, I mean. You get more and more imaginative, and she gets crosser and crosser. I'm sorry, Francis.'

'Truly, Pru, you needn't be, I haven't enjoyed myself so much since the day I was born. And Annaple wasn't willing to marry me anyway, so I haven't lost anything.' He walked into the parlour. 'Good morning, sir. Good morning, Nan. Have you put on your dancing shoes? I'm hoping you'll allow me to partner you at the noon dancing.'

'I'm not in the mood today.'

'Very romantic thing, dancing. You used to say you wanted to be like that girl in the fairytale, the one who danced the soles out of her slippers.'

'Francis.' Annaple took a deep breath. 'I don't know if this is your idea of a joke, but I am getting very tired of it. It's ridiculous, quite ridiculous. It's—it's a *siege*.'

Francis said, 'But you used to tell me how romantic you thought a siege would be. And I haven't put an army round the house, you know. Nor cut off supplies. You can go out whenever you like.'

'I can't, you know I can't, with people gossiping—making up songs about me—'

'That's very romantic too, I'd have thought.'

'It's a siege,' Annaple said again, waving the bread-knife at him.

'Well, you could always surrender.'

'I am *not* going to surrender.'

'Or you could throw boiling oil from the windows. Or milk, if you'd rather. You'll like today's present.'

'I don't want today's present. Or any more presents at all.'

'But it's all arranged.'

'Then un-arrange it.'

'No, no,' Francis said cheerfully. 'You enjoy it really. All your letters say how pleased you are. I'd almost forgotten—look, Nan, today's present isn't exactly—well, tangible, so I've brought round a few oddments to go with it.'

He pulled parcels out of his coat pockets. Annaple began, 'Oh, but Francis—' and then, looking from his face to the ribboned packages, and back again, said help-lessly, 'Thank you. Thank you, Francis.'

She opened the packages: six dozen curtain rings, a packet of pins, an embroidery frame, a pair of scissors, a bag crammed with silk scraps—'So that you can start work on that patchwork quilt you've been talking about, Nan—'

A burst of laughter and applause from the street cut him short. Nine o'clock began to strike. Francis went over to the window, and Prudence, James, and Christopher ran after him. Papa filled his pipe and began to smoke comfortably. After a moment Annaple walked across to the opposite corner of the window.

'*More* swans,' she said limply.

'But you always told me you loved that fairytale.'

'That didn't mean I wanted twenty-one swans on my doorstep.'

Seven swans came floating up the gutter, great white wings curved back, heads travelling high on proud necks. Down the street came sixteen milkmaids leading sixteen cows. Up from the Market Place came the messengers and the workmen with their daily deliveries of fowls, gold rings, wine and birds and flowers.

'What's the cobbler doing here?' Annaple said suspiciously.

'I thought you might need some new dancing shoes.'

'My old ones are perfectly good, and anyway—'

'Just half a dozen pairs. Blue for you and green for

Prudence. And some new buckles for the boys. And a pair of dairymaid's pattens.'

'Oh, *Francis*—What's that?' She pointed at a bundle of sacking which a workman was wheeling on a barrow.

'Oh. Well, that's just a little extra. Something one of my sea-captains picked up in Italy. Just a fountain, Nan, with bronze mermaids and things—I thought it would look nice in the middle of the pond.'

'Listen,' Annaple said. 'Just listen. The courtyard is already crammed with livestock and coops and runs—the woodshed's been turned into a cornbin, you can't get near the well because of all the hens and partridges, the geese make messes everywhere, the water-butts are full of milk, I've had to hang the wash-ing round the kitchen because I can't reach the washing line—'

'Oh, listen,' Prudence begged. 'Can't you hear—surely that's music? But usually the dancing isn't till noon—'

The choir marched up the street, playing their special ninth-day piece, the Dancing Day carol, on flute, recorder, serpent, violin, and clarinet. The crowd began to sing and clap in time.

'Tomorrow shall be my dancing day:
I would my true love did so chance
To see the legend of my play,
To call my true love to my dance:

Sing O my love, O my love, my love, my love;
This have I done for my true love.'

'Oh, Francis—it isn't dancing bears, is it?' Annaple asked in horror.

'No, no. But if you'd like some dancing bears, I'm sure I could—'

'There is nothing, absolutely nothing, that I should like less.'

'Oh, Nan—' Christopher began.

'Kit, be quiet, do.'

The choir formed up. Will Verney's voice rang out sweetly in the second verse.

'Then was I born of a virgin pure,
Of her I took fleshly substance;
Thus was I knit to man's nature,
To call my true love to my dance:
Sing O my love, O my love, my love, my love;
This have I done for my true love.'

'Oh, look!' Prudence called, craning out of the window. 'How lovely!'

Nine ladies were dancing up the street, skirts held out, toes pointed. They wore red bodices, red-flowered skirts looped up over green petticoats, red silk stockings, and shoes with high red heels. The crowd began to clap and stepped back to leave a wide-ish space in the middle of the street. The ladies moved into a slow and stately

dance. Their skirts swung like great nets in a sea-swell, their hair flowed back as if it were spreading out on the water, their cheeks were still and cool like shells. The clapping died away and the crowd held its breath. No one spoke, no one moved. Prudence could hardly bear to watch; and when at last the ladies sank into stillness, there was an instant of complete silence before the applause burst out. Annaple, though she clapped politely, and smiled when the ladies made a final curtsy to her window, said furiously to Francis, 'I hope you're not expecting me to turn this house upside-down fitting in beds for your lady-friends. There isn't an inch of space to spare. Unless, of course, they're willing to double up with the chickens.'

Francis grinned. 'They're staying at the Pig and Whistle.'

The choir struck up the Dancing Day carol all over again. The ladies joined hands and skipped in a circle. The crowd broke up into small groups and copied them, swinging in rings all over the street. By the time they reached the third verse everyone was singing, even Annaple.

> 'In a manger laid and wrapped I was,
> So very poor, this was my chance,
> Betwixt an ox and a silly poor ass,
> To call my true love to my dance—'

Annaple's small, flat voice broke off abruptly and she pressed her hands to her blazing cheeks when she saw Francis grinning at her as he sang the refrain:

'Sing O my love, O my love, my love, my love,
This have I done for my true love.'

Annaple moved quickly away from the window, sure that everyone had seen her furious blushes. Francis followed her.

'Will you be my partner at the noon dancing, Nan?'

'I shan't be going,' Annaple said. 'Nine partridges, sixteen turtle doves, twenty-one hens, two dozen songbirds, two dozen geese, and twenty-one swans take a great deal of looking after.'

* * *

'Not that she does any of it,' Christopher remarked some hours later, when the noon dancing was over and all the streets deserted. Prudence was watering the window boxes and the pear trees, Annaple was curdling milk-and-onion soup in the kitchen, and James and he had been sent to clean out the stream. He scooped out some soggy crusts and flourished his broom at a threatening swan. 'It's us that have to do all the cleaning and feeding and mucking out,' he said.

12

Adam's Day

On the morning of Adam's Day Prudence had her bath in milk.

'What's it like?' Christopher asked her.

'Odd. You feel like a sugar lump—waiting to dissolve. You keep watching your edges to see if they're going soft.'

Annaple came briskly up the stairs. 'Christopher, I've heated up another potful of milk, and your tub's ready in the kitchen. James should be out by now. Mind you wash properly, and give your knees a good scrub. And the back of your neck too.'

'On Adam's Day,' Christopher said bitterly, 'I thought it was treats all round for the men of the house? So my treat's no bath. And could we please have something *not* eggs for breakfast?'

'You can go without breakfast if you like.' Annaple swept out.

'I do wish she'd get married,' Christopher said. 'It's a pity she isn't enjoying all this, like Francis.'

'Francis is quite altered, isn't he? Watch out for the soap,' she called after him, as he set off for the kitchen. 'If you lose it in the milk, it's terribly difficult to find.'

James, coming upstairs to help her uncover the bird-cages, said he hadn't felt like a sugar lump at all. 'More like a drowned fly. Annaple came to check on my ears and ducked my head right under. Where on earth are we going to put today's delivery? Not the chickens and things—there's room for them—but the doves and the birds?'

'Goodness knows.'

Like everyone else in town the Kitsons now had breakfast half an hour earlier. It was traditional to eat apples on Adam's Day, and since this was the kind of tradition Annaple liked, she had cooked apple pancakes. 'Using up the eggs and milk, I see, my dear,' Papa said. 'Is there any lemon?'

'No lemon,' Prudence said. 'Because Nan is being so uppity about going to the market. Only oranges. And they're a bit battered—they're the Mayor's handout ones, Christopher rescued them from the waterspouts.'

The bell rang. Christopher dashed downstairs, but it was only a messenger with a letter from the Mayor. Miss Annaple Kitson's swans were blocking the stream, disturbing the peace, and obstructing the traffic: would she please take the appropriate measures to deal with the nuisance? If not, greatly as the Mayor would regret it, some kind of fine must be imposed.

Annaple dipped her pen in the inkwell and wrote at

a spitting rate: *Miss Kitson presents her compliments to the Mayor, and begs to inform him that the swans to which he refers in his amiable note are the responsibility of Mr Vere.*

The crowd was gathering outside. Neighbours whose windows overlooked the street were hiring out places— 'Excellent views, comfortable chairs, and a cup of apple juice on the house.' The choir arrived early and began to play a selection of carols, while a small fife player went round with a cap for pennies. Some of the women were collecting swansdown for stuffing their pillows and trimming their bodices. Christopher and James struggled out with a tub of milk—'I do hope that isn't Christopher's bath water,' Prudence said doubtfully— and people queued up to dip cupfuls. Presently Christopher rushed out again with a bag of apples and a bundle of forks, and in a few minutes had organized a game of apple-bobbing. A man was selling hot pies, another set up a charcoal stove and began to fry sausages, a third, with a tray of toffee apples round his neck, shouted, 'Two a penny! Two a penny!' The Mayor, always on the watch for a quick shilling, sent his men along with stools from the Town Hall. 'Halfpenny a seat! Watch in comfort! Halfpenny a seat!'

'Free enterprise,' said Papa, who had drawn up his chair and was sitting by the window in a comfortable haze of best French wine and tobacco smoke.

'It looks like a cross between the Goose Fair and the Dairy Day,' Annaple said helplessly.

Christopher said, 'Next year, we'll be able to enter for both.'

* * *

When nine o'clock chimed, people were craning from every window and the street was packed.

'Here they come!' someone shouted. 'Look, they're coming!'

Seven more swans sailing up the gutter. Twenty-four milkmaids leading their cows. Goosegirls and geese. Men with doves and hens and birds. A boy with a box of rings. A man clasping a pear tree. Wine and candied fruit for Papa. Stone jars of preserves, a basket of nuts, a barrel of salted herrings, an enormous pigeon pie, three sacks of apples, and a great round cheese. A couple of stone gargoyles that had caught Francis's fancy. A new clothes line, two fishermen to put it up, a pair of linen baskets, and three dozen clothes pegs. Francis himself, with a sprig of holly in his buttonhole and an apple in his hand. Eighteen dancing ladies—the nine red-flowered ones from the day before, and nine more with black lace shawls cascading from high combs in their hair, deep flounces round their hems, and flowers tucked behind their ears. And last of all, ten extraordinary men. They wore scarlet quilted jackets with wide belts, knee-length boots, and black fur caps; and they were leaping around like hares in March.

'Holy Maria!' James said, hanging right out of the window. 'I wish I could do that.'

The men limbered up with a display of handsprings and cartwheels, did a series of flip-flaps round the crowd and a little elegant juggling with apples, and then wove through a merry Grand Chain with the ladies, throwing in an occasional somersault to keep it lively. 'Different from dancing class!' Christopher said longingly.

The dance grew quicker and wilder, with back somersaults from the lords, dramatic heel-stamping from the ladies, flowers tossed to the crowd, apples spinning in the air. The watchers began to sway with the music, beat time, shake back their hair, jounce their children. The sunlight wavered on the walls, the stream glinted in the

gutter, birds hopped on the roof-trees, swans flew up
with a thump of great white wings, children skipped,
grown-ups swayed, the dancers danced faster and faster,
the musicians blew harder, and as the choir began to sing
the day's carol, there was a sudden lilting in the street,
like a field of barley caught up in a single gust of wind,
and everyone burst out singing.

'Adam lay y-bounden, bounden in a bond;
Four thousand winter thought he not too long.
And all was for an apple, an apple that he took,
As clerkès finden written in their book—'

'If it had been Francis,' Prudence said, waving to him, 'he'd have given *you* the apple, Nan. And probably a whole orchard to go with it.'

'And a few ladders, and a duck pond with decorative ducks—'

'And a couple of sacks of daisy seed, a rustic chair, a trug, a big straw hat—'

'A preserving pan, a tub of cloves—'

'A cider press and a hundred casks.'

The crowd swung into the second verse.

> 'Ne had the apple taken been, the apple taken been,
> Ne had never Our Lady a-been heavenè queen.
> Blessèd be the time that apple taken was.
> Therefore we moun singen Deo gracias.'

There was a roar of applause, some more rose-throwing, and another display of somersaults. The crowd began to sing all over again. But this time they were singing a new version.

> 'Francis lay y-bounden, bounden in a bond;
> Four thousand winter thought he not too long.
> And all was for ANNAPLE, ANNAPLE that he loves,
> And so he sent her a partridge and two doves—'

'Oh, *no*,' Annaple said, appalled, moving back from the window.

'Three hens, four birds, and five gold rings,
Six geese and seven swans,
Eight dairymaids, a dancing troupe,
Ten lords like willow wands.
Blessèd be the girl whose love so merry was,
Therefore she moun singen Deo gracias.'

Annaple didn't think this was romantic at all. 'All the town gossips giving me advice, lecturing me, singing sermons, bandying my affairs in public,' she said; and flounced down to the kitchen to throw together a horrible meal: a sad Yorkshire pudding with bits of burnt herring in it, and a custard on which she sprinkled dried beef instead of ground nutmeg. Then she went off to her bedroom to twang the harp and feel sorry for herself. Prudence, James, and Christopher washed the dishes in hot milk and filled up on apples.

13

Eve's Day

Eve's Day meant treats for the women of the
house, figgy pudding for dinner, wreaths of
green leaves for the girls' heads, and the carol
singers round yet again. 'Oh my goodness, here they
come,' Annaple said, as she heard the singing in the
street. 'Surely they're excessively early? It isn't half past
seven yet, and usually they don't come until at least ten.'

'They have to come round early,' James explained,
'because Francis's presents take up so much of the
morning.'

The doorbell rang, and he opened the window. The
children in the street began to sing. They had high clear
voices, fresh and piercing.

> 'We wish you a merry Christmas, we wish you a
>   merry Christmas,
> We wish you a merry Christmas, and a happy
>   New Year.
> Good tidings we bring to you and your kin.

We wish you a merry Christmas and a happy
    New Year.
For we all like figgy pudding, for we all like figgy
    pudding,
For we all like figgy pudding, so bring some out
    here.
And we won't go till we've got some,
And we won't go till we've got some,
And we won't go till we've got some,
So bring some out here—'

Usually Annaple laughed, and threw pennies from the
window, and said how delightful it was to hear the children's voices; but today she cut them short, sending
Prudence and Christopher down to hand out eggs and
jugs of milk. 'And ask them—*tell* them—please to go
away. My head is aching, I shall have to put wool in my
ears.'

The children, startled at getting eggs and milk instead
of figs and pennies—'Think yourselves lucky it *isn't* her
fearful figgy pudding,' Christopher told them—trooped
off to the end of the street. Their voices sounded faintly
in the distance. The crowd was beginning to gather.

By half past eight the street was like a fairground.
People had come in from nearby villages to watch the
fun. A gingerbread seller arrived. The man with the
charcoal stove was selling hot chestnuts today as well as
sausages. Some men propped up slates and began taking
bets. 'Five to one on dancing ponies.' 'I'll give you three

to one on a pheasant in a fig tree.' 'Five to three on Persian cats.' 'Ten to one on a maypole all complete.' Annaple sniffed. 'Excessively vulgar,' she said.

'What's for breakfast?'

'I'll give you three guesses.'

'Eggs.'

'Yes. Coddled today.'

'Why don't you make French pancakes? You've got the eggs, you've got the milk—'

'Don't mention the word French to me.'

'I thought *you* thought French things were so romantic.'

The crowd began to sing. '*On the* FIRST *day of Christmas my true love sent to me*—' Annaple sliced bread savagely. The children looked at one another and kept quiet. What with the street-cries and the chatter and the singing, the dogs barking excitedly, a baby wailing, the honking geese and the angry hens in the courtyard, and the birds twittering and the bells clinking all around the parlour itself, Prudence could hardly hear Christopher's request for the butter.

As soon as breakfast was over, Prudence and James and Christopher ran across to the window, flung it open and leaned out. Papa lit his morning pipe. Annaple, humming airily to herself, strolled over to the window and sat on the sill, with her back to the street, fidgeting with her embroidery.

'Here they come!' Christopher shouted suddenly. 'Just look—a whole herd of cows!'

Annaple, embroidering white pear blossom on ivory silk, refused to turn her head.

'Here come the dancers—do look, Nan, they're so pretty.'

The ladies came dancing up the street in threes: there were twenty-seven of them today. Following them came twenty lords, leapfrogging over one another's backs.

'They say those ladies in black lace are Spanish,' Papa remarked, drawing his chair over to the window. 'Terrible tempers—jealous, you know. There was nearly a fight at the Pig and Whistle last night, they say. I might

113

stroll down there tonight.' He caught sight of the look on Annaple's face, and added, 'You get a very nice glass of sherry at the Pig and Whistle.'

'There is enough wine in this house to float a ship,' Annaple retorted.

'Listen!' Christopher leant out dangerously far, and James grabbed his belt. 'Can't you hear it? It's—it's *drums*.'

'Drums?' Annaple dropped her embroidery. 'Oh goodness, what crazy idea can he have got hold of now?'

'Cavalry?' Christopher suggested hopefully. 'A troop of cavalry?'

'Here comes Francis,' Prudence said. She waved to him.

Francis was making his way through the crowd. The lords bowed, the ladies blew him kisses, the milkmaids looked up from their pails, the goosegirls bobbed curtsies. 'Good morning, good morning,' Francis said cheerfully, as he passed. 'Merry Christmas.' He looked up to the parlour window. 'Hello, Pru. My compliments to Nan, and I'm bringing up my army.'

The sound of the drums grew steadily louder. Eleven drummer boys came marching up the street. The gilded cords on the drums swayed, heavy with tassels. Scarlet sashes rippled, gold fringes dangled against scarlet cloth. Annaple was so afraid there might be soldiers behind the drummers that she swallowed her pride and leant out of the window. Not soldiers: something worse. She put her hand to her mouth. A cannon. A small bronze cannon being towed by four fisherboys. The crowd shouted, 'Going to war, Francis? Mislaid your army? Watch out which way you point that thing. Will it really fire?'

'Certainly it will fire,' Francis replied. 'Not only will it fire, it is going to.'

The older people drew back, the small boys pressed nearer, the mothers reached for their children. The fisherboys towed the cannon into a position directly facing the Kitsons' house and tilted the barrel so that it pointed straight at the parlour window. Annaple stood her ground, but she looked nervous.

'Do you think he's really going to fire it?' whispered Prudence.

'I do *hope* so,' Christopher said.

Down in the street no one breathed. Francis signalled to the drummers. They began a long roll on the drums. He stepped forward to light the fuse. The small bright flame crept towards the barrel. A steady ruffle of drums filled the street. Annaple was breathing sharply, as though she had been running a race, but she stood still. The last inch of fuse burned away, the drummers swung their sticks up in salute, and the cannon fired. Figs and sweetmeats and paper flowers shot into the air and showered over the street. Annaple, who had instinctively flung up her hands, was bombarded with sugar plums. She said angrily, 'Really, if Francis thinks this is funny—!' Christopher and James collapsed in laughter. The crowd, at first astonished, began to laugh and clap.

Children scrambled for the sweetmeats. Francis, looking pleased with himself, signalled to the drummers again, and they marched through some exhibition figures, turning as neatly as clockwork, with a great many twirls and flourishes.

'Very trim,' Papa said. 'Very trim indeed. Most soldierly.'

'Oh, I think it's glorious.' Christopher leant out of the window. 'I wish I was old enough to be a soldier. Look, Nan, isn't it romantic?'

'No.'

'Where's my trumpet?'

'Wherever you put it. I'm always telling you to put your toys away.'

'It isn't a toy. It's real.'

Francis looked up at Annaple.

'If you came down now,' he called, 'we could have a drumhead wedding.'

116

'Thank you. No.'

'You said you enjoyed the Summer Review so much. You said it was wonderfully romantic.'

'I seem to have said a great many things I now regret,' Annaple retorted. 'I hope you're intending to take your cannon away. If you leave it there, I shall be getting notes from the Mayor demanding Gun Parking Fees.'

'I thought it would look rather fine,' Francis said, giving the barrel a cheerful slap. 'Give the house an air.'

To this Annaple made no reply at all. Francis signalled to the drummers, and they began to rap out the beat of the new Christmas song. The choir began to sing. '*On the* ELEVENTH *day of Christmas, my true love sent to me*—' Christopher rushed out of the front door, blowing on his trumpet. The crowd began to clap and sing, the ladies shook out their skirts and danced, the lords

turned cartwheels, the goosegirls and the milkmaids skipped in time. Annaple, watching from her window, saw them all forming up in procession. At the head was Christopher, blowing shrilly on his trumpet. Then Francis looking pleased with himself, the drummers, the choir, the lords wildly leaping, the ladies dancing, the swans floating downstream, the goosegirls, a line of geese, the workmen, the messengers and the errand boys, the milkmaids swinging their pails, the cows jiggling along, the musicians, husbands and wives arm-in-arm, old women with their knitting, mothers with their babies, little boys with penny whistles, little girls bowling hoops, old men hobbling on sticks, and last of all, running to catch up as the procession danced away down the street, Prudence and James, hand in hand, and Papa strolling down to the Pig and Whistle.

Annaple watched them all dance merrily away, leaving her alone with a houseful of twittering birds and a courtyard crammed with cross fowls. The roar of the singing and the throb of the drums faded in the distance. Annaple looked down at the deserted street, sighed, and went downstairs to fetch in the milk.

14

Twelfth Night

Annaple sniffed, seeing the crowded street, and said, 'Perhaps after today Francis will leave me alone.'

The children looked at one another and sighed.

The crowd was turning all one way, as if a wind blew it. Shouts could be clearly heard above the babble. 'Here they come! Look, just turning up from the Market Place.'

'I can hear drums!' Christopher shouted.

As the procession came marching up the street, the choir began to sing. '*On the* FIRST *day of Christmas my true love sent to me—*' The crowd roared the refrains.

A boy with a pear tree, the topheavy partridge swaying in its branches. A man with two turtle doves cooing in their cage. ('Christopher, I suppose you had better run down and let them in.') A man holding the last batch of French hens, all squawking angrily. A boy with four robins. Another boy with a box of rings. Six goosegirls carrying six geese. Seven black-masked swans sailing up the gutter to tug at the doorbell. ('If this is how a mother bird feels,' Prudence said, showering bread to forty-two greedy beaks, 'I sympathize.') Forty milkmaids leading forty cows. (Annaple covered her face with her hands.) Thirty-six ladies dancing along. Thirty lords leaping like schoolboys. Twenty-two drummers with scarlet sashes and gilt-tasselled drums.

The noise was tremendous: the drums, the honking geese, strange shouts from the leapfrogging lords, the mooing cows, the whistling birds, the choir still singing, the musicians still playing, and voices asking ceaselessly, 'What is it? What has he sent today? Can you see? What *is* it?'

Annaple bowed to Francis, who was standing under the window looking hopefully up at her. Then she put her hands over her ears and closed her eyes. She said, 'What is it, Prudence? Tell me quickly.'

'But I can't *see*—everyone's jumping and pushing down in the street—Kit, can *you* see? Whatever is it?'

Unexpectedly the crowd fell quiet. Everyone stood still, heads cocked, listening. The choir broke off its singing; the drummers stopped drumming; the milk-maids checked in the middle of milking. The street was perfectly silent.

They could all hear it now: a strange wailing sound in the distance, high and shrill, like the wind screaming on the cliffs. It was coming nearer. Annaple took her hands from her ears and stood, amazed. The lament filled the

air. The crowd was too astonished to move. Then a cat
screeched and leapt for the nearest drainpipe, and as if
this had shattered the spell people moved hurriedly
backwards, cramming themselves into doorways and
flattening themselves against the house walls. The ladies
cried out and the lords sprang, trying to see. The drummers formed a stiff military square and waited with
drumsticks upraised. The cows were tossing their heads
and mooing in fright, and the milkmaids were crying
that the milk would be ruined. 'It will turn sour—all
those bucketfuls wasted!' The day's delivery of geese
jumped from their nests and lined up for battle, hissing
furiously. The hens set up a terrified squawking. There
was a snow flurry of feathers as the great cloud of swans
flew up to the rooftops. People began to whisper, 'What
is it? What can it be?'

'It's souls in torment, I tell you, souls in torment.'

'It's the Day of Judgement, it's the end of us all—'

Christopher was now standing on the sill and leaning
out, figurehead style, his hands gripping the window
frame. 'There are men coming,' he called. 'Up from the
Market—men in *skirts*—I can't exactly see—they're
blowing up footballs or something—balloons with
spokes sticking out—'

'It's bagpipes!' Annaple cried suddenly. 'Scottish bagpipes!'

'It's enough to turn a man's stomach to water,' Papa
said, 'and curdle the eggs in their shells.'

Prudence and James stared at Annaple in amazement.

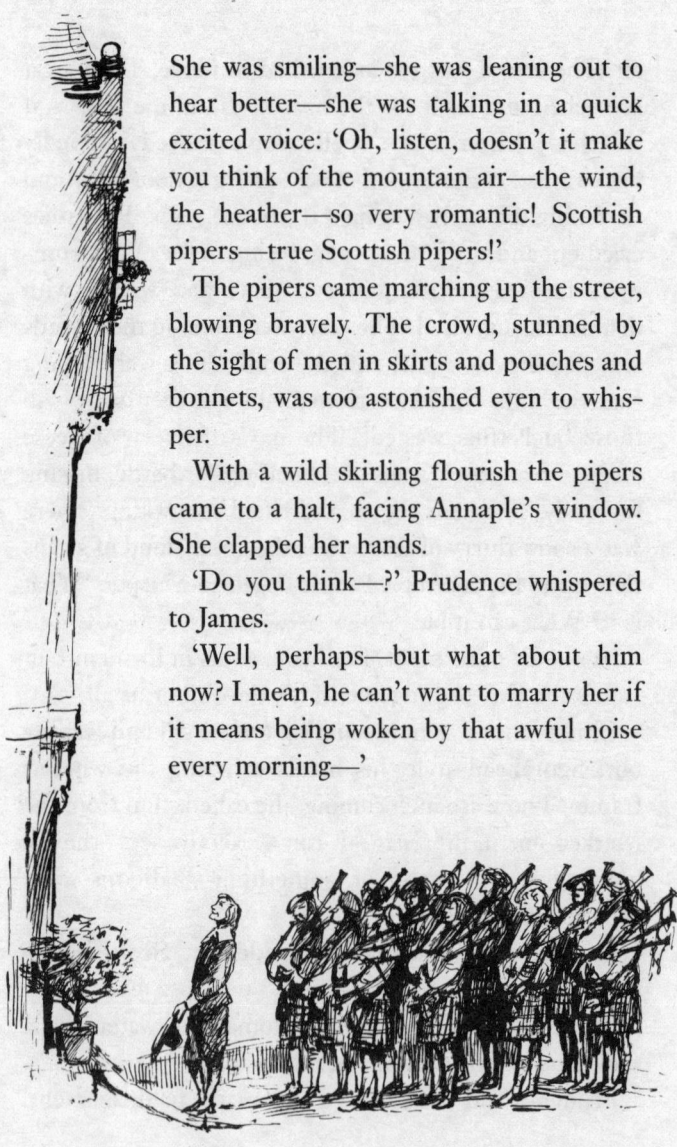

She was smiling—she was leaning out to hear better—she was talking in a quick excited voice: 'Oh, listen, doesn't it make you think of the mountain air—the wind, the heather—so very romantic! Scottish pipers—true Scottish pipers!'

The pipers came marching up the street, blowing bravely. The crowd, stunned by the sight of men in skirts and pouches and bonnets, was too astonished even to whisper.

With a wild skirling flourish the pipers came to a halt, facing Annaple's window. She clapped her hands.

'Do you think—?' Prudence whispered to James.

'Well, perhaps—but what about him now? I mean, he can't want to marry her if it means being woken by that awful noise every morning—'

Francis looked up at the parlour window. 'Annaple, are you—pleased?'

'Yes, yes, of course. I've always wanted to be woken by pipers. It's the most delightful surprise ever.'

Christopher whispered, 'She's pleased, really pleased—'

'Perhaps if we ran down and let him in—then when everyone's gone, we could call Papa down to the kitchen—Nan just might say yes—'

But Francis was past considering the crowd. 'Nan—' he said. 'Nan—'

'Oh, not now,' Prudence whispered in anguish. 'Not with everyone listening, she'll be furious—'

Francis swallowed. He began again, 'Annaple—'

Annaple said, 'Yes. If you still want me to.'

In the astonished silence, Prudence stared at her sister and thought she looked as taken aback as everyone else.

Francis said, 'Nan, do you mean—*Nan*—' And then, determined to put it plainly, 'Anne, will you marry me?'

Annaple blushed, but she put up her chin. 'Yes,' she said. 'I will.'

* * *

For the rest of the day the children tiptoed around, being so good that Papa asked if they were feeling quite well.

'Just cautious about believing it, Papa.'

'She couldn't change her mind now, could she?'

'Couldn't she just!' Christopher said. 'I shan't feel sure of it until I see the ring—rings?—on her finger.'

But when Francis came round that evening for the Twelfth Night supper, he brought with him a marriage licence from the Bishop. Everything, he said, was ready for a wedding next day. He had booked the bell-ringers, the organist, the choir, and the church; he had informed the uncles—'Five rings, I promised, so that they can bless one each'; he had got the Mayor's permission; he had ordered the wedding feast from the Pig and Whistle; and he had invited the guests, which was easy since everyone was coming. 'In fact,' he added, grinning, 'all the people who came in from the villages to watch the fun this morning are staying in town overnight so that they can take in the wedding as well.'

'But, Francis—'

'Whatever will you wear, Nan? Perhaps we could trim your Sunday dress—'

'There's no need for that—unless, of course, you want to, Nan,' Francis said. 'I went down to the draper's and bought up his stock—a dozen yards of white lawn, a dozen yards of white silk, ribbons in every colour he had, thread, needles, hooks, pins, lacing—'

'Oh, Francis!'

'—and the dressmakers are coming round after supper to measure you and talk about patterns and all that kind of thing—they've said they'll sit up all night if need be—and I've bought a dress for you, Pru, only a ready-made one, I'm afraid, and I had to guess at your size—well, actually, I bought three, so one should be sure to fit—'

'*Francis*—'

'—green, I thought that was a colour you liked—there should be time to get one of them trimmed, shouldn't there? Trimmed, and taken in or let out or whatever? I bought a lot of different trimmings so that you could choose one you liked. Is there anything I've forgotten?'

'Nothing, you've been wonderful, but—well, isn't it all rather a hurry?'

'I thought you'd find a whirlwind wedding more romantic,' explained Francis, who was learning fast.

Then Prudence fetched the Twelfth Night cake, which was one of Annaple's soggier efforts, and Christopher blew out the three candles and cut slices for them all. Annaple got the slice with the bean in it, which made her ruler of the evening. 'I ought,' she said, 'to make the most of this—tell James to cut his nails, for instance, and Papa to give up smoking that pipe, and Christopher to wash his hair, and Prudence to darn her stockings—but I don't want to make myself that easy to say goodbye to. *Really* tomorrow, Francis?'

'Really tomorrow.'

15

The Feast of the Three Kings

On the morning of the Three Kings Feast, which was Christopher's birthday as well as Annaple's wedding day, Francis sent the twelve pipers to wake his bride. They marched up Lee Street blowing bravely on their pipes, waking not only the bride, but her father and sister and brothers as well, all the livestock—which squawked and hissed and cackled in horror—and everyone else in the street. 'Holy Maria!' Prudence said. She shot bolt upright in bed and grabbed for the blankets too late. 'I thought I was having a nightmare. Nan, do call out to them to stop.'

But Annaple, already out of bed and reaching for her wrapper, only said, 'You'd better get up, we've a great deal to do. Listen, isn't it romantic?'

Prudence, now standing on her bed to try to catch the doves, which had been frightened clear out of their cages, said crossly, 'No, not a bit.' Annaple, humming the lament off-key, went downstairs to hang the biggest cooking pot over the fire and fill it with milk for baths.

The children were so pleased at the idea of a starchless, buttonless future, filled with delightful meals sent up from the Pig and Whistle, that they washed their hair and had their baths and cut their nails without a murmur; and Papa, having shaved with hot milk (which worked up, he said, a very creamy lather), peacefully allowed Annaple to trim his hair and tie his cravat, instead of protesting that he was a grown man, not a babe in arms, and needed no help in dressing himself, especially not from flibbertigibbet daughters.

The messengers began to arrive soon after seven o'clock. Flowers for Annaple. Flowers for Prudence. Buttonholes for Papa and James and Christopher. ('Put them in water, James—*water*—they don't like milk, it turns them waxy.') Annaple's wedding dress. Prudence's bridesmaid dress. A new cravat pin for Papa. Trays of breakfast from the Pig and Whistle. ('*Look*,' James said, lifting the lids to find bacon and sausages and mushrooms, porridge, cream and candied raspberries, hot new bread wrapped in a napkin, butter, preserves, slices of pink ham, cold roast beef, milk and ale and wine. 'Quick, Kit, come and look at this!') A note from the Mayor presenting his compliments to Annaple and pointing out that a fee must be paid for the Blocking of the Market Place by Marriage Traffic. 'He'd really like to bring in a law that would let him charge people for parking their carts,' James said. 'So much per wheel.'

'So much per hoof too,' Papa said.

Annaple smiled. 'I shall walk to my wedding.'

Francis sent a basket of oranges and lemons, a box of candied apricots, a small frangipani tree in a red pot, a honeycomb, a seal ring and a dozen sticks of sealing wax, a diamond-headed pencil for writing on glass, and a note saying, '*Some bits and pieces I picked up over Christmas and didn't have a chance to send round before.*' He also sent a yellow silk sash, a handspan wide and twice as long as a man, with a note pinned to it: '*This was once my father's sash, he wore it in his soldiering days, I thought the colour might please you; he would have liked you to have it.*'

The five uncles arrived and kissed the bride, ate two goose eggs each, tasted the French wine—'Excellent, quite excellent'—and went off to the church. Aunt Rachel came, kissed everyone, and said how much this reminded her of her sister Elizabeth's wedding day. James, who was to be best man, tipped all forty rings into his pocket—'I think I'd better take them all, it would be so awful to take just one and lose it'—and ran off to Green Street, his pocket banging against his knee and clinking at every step. Annaple confiscated Christopher's penny whistle. 'But, Nan,' he protested, 'it's nowhere near as shrill as those awful pipes you moon over.' The geese and hens and partridges were squawking so loudly for breakfast that Prudence ran down in her petticoat and showered corn over the court-yard until it lay inches deep in the coops. The swans, upset by the bagpipes, had taken to the rooftops and were blowing about up there, rattling the tiles and nibbling at the moss. The doves and the songbirds got in everyone's way, pecking at Christopher's toes as he hopped around looking for his shoes, and catching their claws in Prudence's hair, still damp from its early washing. The Verneys arrived to take Aunt Rachel down to the church with them, and she kissed Annaple again and went, murmuring, 'Dear child, I can see you're going to be late—I'll have a word with the choirmaster.'

At twenty to eleven Annaple was searching frantically for her gloves. 'Where in the world have they gone?'

'I expect you've put them somewhere safe,' Prudence said, meaning to be helpful.

'They're wherever you put them,' Christopher said solemnly, 'they can't get up and walk, you know. Dear me, we're always telling you to put your things away.' But in spite of his teasing, he joined in the search.

'Can't you go without them, Nan?'

'Not to *church*—' Annaple began; but then she grew calmer and said, 'Well, yes, of course I can. Gloves aren't really important.'

'You could have your mother's if you liked,' Papa said unexpectedly. 'I think they're still in her coffer, where she left them. But they're old, of course. Discoloured, I expect.'

Prudence expected Annaple to say hurriedly that it was nice of him to think of it, but really, she could perfectly well go without; but instead she said, '*Mama's* gloves—oh, yes.'

'I'll fetch them. You'd better go up and dress, my dear.'

Annaple's dress was made out of white lawn over white silk. Stitched into the bodice were the strips of ivory silk on which, in her more fanciful moments, she had painfully embroidered sprigs of white pear blossom and small green leaves. The cuffs and collar were edged with narrow lace, once white but now ivory with age; Aunt Rachel had sent it round. The gloves had been white when Mama carried them to her wedding, but now they too were yellowish-ivory and smelt of the lavender in which they had lain for twenty years.

Annaple laced up her bodice; shook out skirts and cuffs; and tied round her waist the sash that had belonged to Francis's soldier father. Its deep fringed ends fell to the hem of her dress. She unpinned her braided hair. She hadn't worn it loose since her fifteenth birthday. It was newly-washed, thick and shining, with ripples in it from the braiding, and reached below her waist, Prudence stepped up on a stool to brush and pin it for her, and then took the ring of Christmas roses and ivy and set it carefully on her sister's head.

Annaple picked up her posy. She looked questioningly at Prudence, who looked back and said shyly, 'You look like—like narcissus, Nan.' Annaple bent forward and kissed her.

Then in a moment the old Annaple was back: 'Pru, quick, you must get dressed, you can't be a bridesmaid in your petticoat.'

Prudence pulled the green dress over her head, hooked herself into it, tied the bodice ribbons, shook out the lace cuffs, and squashed her feet into her new soft green leather shoes. Annaple brushed her hair for her and braided it, and then pinned the braids into a crown: they were just long enough. Prudence touched them cautiously; it was the first time she had worn her hair up, and the back of her neck felt cold. Then she jammed her own hoop of flowers on her head and picked up her posy. She was ready.

Downstairs Papa and Christopher were waiting. Annaple looked them over. Papa said, 'You look like Elizabeth. You look like your mother.' He put her green cloak around her shoulders, and Christopher opened the door.

Eleven o'clock chimed from the church tower. Christopher and Prudence, Annaple and Papa, stepped out of the house, crossed the bridge, and turned to walk down Lee Street to the Market Place. The pipers and drummers, sent along by Francis, fell into place in front of and behind them and struck up *God Rest You Merry, Gentlemen*. Annaple said, 'Papa, your pocket is bulging, have you pushed your tobacco pouch into it? Kit, have you remembered your clean handkerchief? Look where you're going, Pru—'

Prudence kept looking up to the rooftops where the swans were standing, wings upraised, flamboyant against the sky.

They came to the Market Place, crossed it, and went into the church, which was crammed to the doors. There was a little narrow lane left for Annaple to walk through. She slipped off her cloak. The guests at the back of the church turned to look and smile. The musicians were playing briskly and jubilantly. Prudence, counting her steps as she followed Papa and Annaple down the aisle, glanced from side to side at the workmen, the messengers, the gravedigger, the carpenter, the shopkeepers and the stall-holders, the fishermen, the sea-captains, the farmers, the Keeper, the tradesmen, the lords and ladies in their strange, brilliant garments, the milkmaids and the goosegirls, the Mayor done up in scarlet with his best chain, the neighbours and the carol singers, Aunt Rachel, the Bishop, the choir, and here, waiting for them, the five uncles in their best clerical black, and Francis, with James beside him.

The Bishop gave the opening address and then stepped back, giving place to the five uncles who put the questions in chorus. Francis and Annaple answered that yes, they did wish to marry one another.

'Who gives this woman to be married to this man?'

'I do,' said Papa.

'Repeat after us,' the uncles said. 'I, Francis Peter—'

'I, Francis Peter . . . '

He sounded as if he couldn't believe it was really happening.

'—for better, for worse, in sickness and in health—'

'Thinking of Nan's cooking,' Christopher whispered cheerfully to Prudence.

'Shush.'

Annaple glanced round to hush Christopher, but just then the uncles began on her vows and she had to face front again.

'Repeat after us. I, Anne Elizabeth—'

'I, Anne Elizabeth . . . '

Prudence held her breath. But Annaple's voice was as small and clear as the bell on Evangelist's Day, and she went steadily through the promises.

'Is it certain yet?' Christopher whispered. Prudence shook her head.

James produced five rings, the uncles blessed one each, and Francis slid all five on to Annaple's finger, which stuck out so stiffly she couldn't bend the knuckle. 'With these rings,' he said, 'I thee wed.'

Christopher whispered, '*Now* is it certain?'

'Not quite yet. Soon.'

Twelve days of present-giving had gone to Francis's head and, unable to resist adding a touch of his own to the ceremony, he now produced from his coat pockets two china jars, one glazed in scarlet and gold, the other sprinkled with white flowers on blue, and put them into Annaple's hands. He lifted the lids. A great sweetness filled the church.

'Because it's Three Kings Day,' he explained. 'The rings are for gold, and in this red and gold jar there's frankincense and in the blue and white one there's myrrh.'

'Francis, how lovely!'

'*If* we may now continue . . . ' an uncle said coldly.

'Oh, of course. I just thought it would add a little extra—'

'I'm so sorry,' Annaple put in, smiling at her uncles.

'Very well then. We do pronounce thee man and wife.'

Prudence and James and Christopher and Papa looked at one another and sighed with relief and happiness and regret.

Then they all knelt down and prayed for Francis and Annaple, and the Bishop blessed first the bridegroom and the bride, and then everyone else in the church. Francis led Annaple into the sacristy, with the five uncles flocking after them, then Papa and Aunt Rachel, then James and Prudence, with Christopher last. Behind them in the church the musicians began to play again and the choirmaster chivvied the choir into one of its carefully practised carols, with an elaborate and difficult descant; but first the drummers and pipers joined in, and then everyone else in the church, so that descant, fiddle, accompaniment and all were swallowed up in a great cheerful roar. The choirmaster sniffed, but Annaple did a little jigging dance as she waited for Francis to hand her the pen so that she could write her girlhood name for the last time: Anne Elizabeth Kitson. Papa signed as one witness and Prudence as the other, and then all the uncles wrote their names very small, squashing all five of them into the place headed 'Clergyman'.

Francis took Annaple's hand and led her back to the sacristy door just as congregation, drummers, pipers and all, ignoring the choirmaster's attempts to conduct, roared out a last alleluia. The musicians sank back, exhausted with the effort to keep up; the congregation collapsed happily into the pews; the choir giggled, the choirmaster looked as yellow and sour as lemon peel; and then silence came down like a snuffer over a candle as Will Verney began to sing.

'The marriage was made in winter
When Mary's son was born;
The marriage was made in springtime
When He was crowned with thorn.

Made it was in Nazareth,
And made in Bethlehem,
And made it was when Jesus rose,
In Jerusalem.

Married were we at Christmas,
And so may merry lie;
Married were we at Easter,
And so shall never die.'

The wedding feast was at the Pig and Whistle. There were rather a lot of egg-and-milk dishes, and a good deal of left-over Twelfth Night cake dressed up as trifle, but everything was beautifully cooked. The ladies gave a dancing display, full of flower-throwing and kiss-blowing; the lords gave a leaping one, rolling in hoops around the floor and then suddenly uncoiling and shooting up to swing from the rafters; and someone poured milk into the bagpipes, which was a relief to everyone but Annaple and the pipers. The uncles proposed the health of the bride and groom. The Mayor kissed Annaple's cheek and said that he hoped she had made arrangements for the livestock accumulated during her courtship.

'I'll buy you a farm, Nan,' Francis said; but Annaple said that Christmas had altered her ideas of simple country life; she had decided that she was a town girl at heart.

The guests, reminded by Francis's words, pulled presents out of their pockets. Francis and Annaple did very well out of this, and Christopher fairly well, since it was his birthday; James and Prudence only got some leftover bits and pieces, but Francis came over and asked if they had decided what they would choose for his wedding presents to them. 'Anything you like,' he said.

James and Prudence looked at one another, wondering if they ought really to ask for, say, a penknife and a pin-cushion. Francis saved them. 'I thought of a boat,' he said to James, 'but if there's anything else you'd rather have—'

James swallowed. 'There's nothing in the world I'd rather have than a boat, but—'

'Excellent. Now, about Christopher—would he like a horse, do you think?'

'He'd be absolutely delighted, only where would we put it?'

'I'll get a stable built. What about you, Pru?'

'Could I—could I have a clock, do you think? A little clock for my bedroom?'

'If that's what you want, yes, of course.' Francis paused. 'A *little* clock?' he said doubtfully.

Prudence thought of grandfather clocks as tall as a man, church clocks, clocks with mechanical figures that processed at the hour. 'Small enough for us to be able to get it up the stairs,' she said.

Francis cheered up at once. There were windows, after all; windows, pulleys, scaffolding; at a pinch one might even take the staircase out altogether, hoist the clock up the stairwell, then put the stairs back in again—'I must see what I can do, Pru.'

Christopher came frisking across the floor. He had been doing sums with cherry stones left over from the trifles. 'Do you realize,' he said, 'that if you add the presents up—leaving out all the oddments, I mean—if you add up twelve partridges, twenty-two doves, thirty French hens, thirty-six birds, forty gold rings, forty-two geese, forty-two swans, forty cows, thirty-six dancing ladies, thirty leaping lords, twenty-two drummers, *and* twelve pipers'—he paused for breath—'then you've got three hundred and sixty-four presents.'

'Well, yes. I suppose so—' Prudence said doubtfully. She didn't even try to check Christopher's arithmetic, but every shopkeeper in the room at once began to do so. Francis, who was quick at figuring after all those hours in the counting-house, got there just ahead of the Mayor. 'Three hundred and sixty-four,' he said, consideringly. 'It's not really a very round number.'

'No,' Annaple said hastily, afraid he might try to make it up to the roundness of five hundred, 'it's more than enough, truly.'

'What I mean *is*,' Christopher said, 'it's a present for every day of the year but one.'

'So it is. What would you like for one last present, sweeting?'

But Annaple only shook her head and said she had it already.

* * *

The feast went on until dusk. Then they all lit lanterns and candles and went out into the Market Place. The church clock began to chime the hour. As the last note died away, the whispers and shiftings in the crowd faded into a listening stillness.

The clop of hooves and the rumble of cartwheels sounded faintly in the distance. The cart trundled slowly down the dark, deserted streets into the crowded Market Place. Prudence saw the dark wedge of the shafts, the glint of turning wheels, the haze of straw heaped up and splaying out in the lantern-light, the ripple of the horse's flanks; and then, as the cart rumbled past her, she saw Mary sitting in the straw, and Joseph beside her, and the baby in Mary's arms.

The cart halted. The three Kings came in slow procession across the Market Place, and the choir began to sing the last of its Christmas carols.

'A little child there is y-born,
Eia, eia, susanni, susanni, susanni.
And he sprang out of Jesse's thorn,
Alleluya, Alleluya.
To save us all that were forlorn.

139

Now Jesus is the childès name,
Eia, eia, susanni, susanni, susanni.
And Mary mild she is his dame;

Alleluya, Alleluya.
And so our sorrow is turned to game.'

The Kings climbed into the cart, put their presents in Mary's lap, and knelt down in the straw.

'Three kings there came with their presents,
Eia, eia, susanni, susanni, susanni,
Of myrrh, and gold and frankincense,
Alleluya, Alleluya.
As clerkès sing in their sequence.

Now sit we down upon our knee,
Eia, eia, susanni, susanni, susanni,
And pray we to the Trinity,
Alleluya, Alleluya.
Our help and succour for to be.'

The last note sang out on the cold air. The men took off their hats and the women and children went down on their knees. The echo of the singing still sounded in their ears. Then the carter clicked his tongue at the horse and shook the reins, and the cart trundled slowly across the Market Place, carrying Mary and Joseph and the Kings away into the darkness. The lantern glimmered, climbing the steep dark street, and then was gone. The clop of the hooves and the rattle of the wheelrims faded into silence.

The crowd shifted and broke up into small gossiping groups. Annaple kissed her father and Prudence, James, and Christopher. 'Now, do remember to clean your teeth—don't forget to change the linen tomorrow—Papa, do be sure to cover the fire before you go to bed—oh, my darlings.'

Francis took her hand, and he and she turned to walk across the Market Place towards Green Street. The drummers beat softly on their drums; people called good wishes; someone blew a few notes in salute on a fife, someone else began to whistle; the fiddler played a note for the choir; and then all the scattered sounds flowed together, and everyone was singing.

'On the first day of Christmas my true love
     sent to me
A partridge in a pear tree.

On the second day of Christmas my true love
     sent to me
Two turtle doves,
And a partridge in a pear tree.

On the third day of Christmas my true love
     sent to me
Three French hens,
Two turtle doves,
And a partridge in a pear tree.'

Still singing, the crowd took partners and formed a long double line, snaking round the Market Place. The couples held up their hands in Orange-and-Lemon arches, and Annaple and Francis stooped, laughing, to run down the tunnel while the voices sang overhead.

'On the fourth day of Christmas my true love
      sent to me
Four calling birds,
Three French hens, two turtle doves,
And a partridge in a pear tree.

On the fifth day of Christmas my true love
      sent to me
Five gold rings,
Four calling birds, three French hens,
      two turtle doves,
And a partridge in a pear tree.

On the sixth day of Christmas my true love
      sent to me
Six geese a-laying,
Five gold rings,
Four calling birds, three French hens,
      two turtle doves,
And a partridge in a pear tree.'

Annaple and Francis emerged, breathless and untidy, and ran up Green Street, hand in hand. The crowd poured after them, bombarding them with paper flowers, and a group of boys dashed past and cut off the way to Francis's house.

'Oh, dear,' Annaple said, laughing and pushing back her tangled hair. 'Do let us through—oh, Jem, please—Kit, won't you let us by?'

But the boys joined hands and danced around Annaple and Francis, keeping them captive. The Mayor came panting up the street and held up his lantern to inspect the drifts of coloured paper in the gutter. 'We'll be getting fines for Wedding Litter in the morning,' Annaple said to Francis; but he only laughed and said he didn't care, and she began to laugh too, and scooped up a great handful of paper flowers to throw at her brothers.

'On the seventh day of Christmas my true love
      sent to me
Seven swans a-swimming,
Six geese a-laying,
Five gold rings,
Four calling birds, three French hens,
      two turtle doves,
And a partridge in a pear tree.

On the eighth day of Christmas my true love
      sent to me
Eight maids a-milking,
Seven swans a-swimming, six geese a-laying,
Five gold rings,
Four calling birds, three French hens,
      two turtle doves,
And a partridge in a pear tree.

On the ninth day of Christmas my true love
      sent to me
Nine ladies dancing,
Eight maids a-milking, seven swans a-swimming,
      six geese a-laying,
Five gold rings,
Four calling birds, three French hens,
      two turtle doves,
And a partridge in a pear tree.'

Francis saw a break in the crowd and ran for it, swinging Annaple after him. They reached his doorstep safely, and he fumbled for the key, pulling his pockets inside out, and found it, and unlocked the door, and turned with Annaple to wave goodbye. Annaple threw her wedding posy to Prudence, and James threw back a small leather bag. 'The other rings,' he called. 'Thirty-five of them. Just in case you mislay the ones you've got on.'

The crowd swung triumphantly into the next verse.

'On the tenth day of Christmas my true love
    sent to me
Ten lords a-leaping,
Nine ladies dancing,
Eight maids a-milking, seven swans a-swimming,
    six geese a-laying,
Five gold rings,
Four calling birds, three French hens,
    two turtle doves,
And a partridge in a pear tree.

On the eleventh day of Christmas my true love
    sent to me
Eleven drummers drumming,
Ten lords a-leaping, nine ladies dancing,
Eight maids a-milking, seven swans a-swimming,
    six geese a-laying,
Five gold rings,

Four calling birds, three French hens,
> two turtle doves,
And a partridge in a pear tree.

On the twelfth day of Christmas my true love
> sent to me
Twelve pipers piping,
Eleven drummers drumming,
Ten lords a-leaping, nine ladies dancing,
Eight maids a-milking, seven swans a-swimming,
> six geese a-laying,
Five gold rings,
Four calling birds, three French hens,
> two turtle doves,
And a partridge in a pear tree.'

Annaple's voice rose unexpectedly. It was flat and uncertain, and her cheeks were blazing, but the words were perfectly clear.

'On the last day of Christmas my true love
> gave to me
His heart to be my own—'

With a great crash of music the crowd joined in, and the last triumphant refrain rolled through the town.

'Twelve pipers piping, eleven drummers
  drumming,
Ten lords a-leaping, nine ladies dancing,
Eight maids a-milking, seven swans a-swimming,
  six geese a-laying,
Five gold rings,
Four calling birds, three French hens,
  two turtle doves,
And a partridge in a pear tree.'

Francis waved, Annaple called, 'Goodbye, goodbye—'
and blew kisses to her family. She began to say
something about supper and using up the cheese, but
Francis laughed, pulled her in, and shut the door.

* * *

'And she's happy, and so's Francis, and she's not
far away, so she can come round and see us, though
I hope she won't be rushing round to check on us
every hour, and we can manage perfectly well for
ourselves, especially with all the meals coming up
from the Pig and Whistle, oh, glory, and I'm going
to have a horse, a real horse, and everything's settled
comfortably. We finally got her married off. We
finally did it.' Christopher lay back triumphantly in his
chair.

'Yes, but I do wish she'd taken the livestock with her.
We've been turned into a couple of farmer's boys. I wonder when my boat will be ready?'

'I wonder when my horse will come?' Christopher slewed round to look at Prudence. 'What did you ask for, Pru?'

'A clock.'

'That's a bit mingy for Francis. He'll probably send a dozen.'

'And a proper ship's chronometer.'

'And a couple of grandfathers, and a sundial or two.'

'And an hourglass,' added Papa, 'and a water clock, and one of those chiming affairs.'

'And every hour, *on* the hour, the house will rock with chimes,' Christopher said cheerfully, rocking his chair.

'Oughtn't you to sit up straight?' Prudence asked doubtfully. 'If the chair slid, you could hurt your back—'

Christopher said firmly, 'No, Pru. Surely we needn't get you married off for several years yet?'

'What do you mean?' Prudence asked suspiciously.

James shook his head. 'I think she's going to begin sounding just like Nan,' he said sadly. '*Don't* tilt your chair—*do* sit up straight—*don't* play with your fork—*do* wash your hair—'

'We'd better get to work on Will Verney.'

James gave a sudden crow of laughter. 'No, we won't. We'll ask Francis. He'll send round a dozen bride-grooms the very next day.'

But Prudence was no longer listening. She said

urgently, 'The Christmas candle's sinking—quick, blow the others out.'

James blew out the candles that stood on the table and the chimney ledge and the window sill. The Kitsons stood in the darkened room watching the last thin slip of Christmas burn away.

As they stood there, they heard the clop of horse's hooves and the rattle of cartwheels as Mary and Joseph travelled slowly through the town towards the Sea Gate. A boy was singing the Egypt carol, unaccompanied, thin and faraway. They heard one broken line as it wavered into earshot, and then a single verse:

'—on Egypt's trackless sand.

Star-led, the kings and shepherds came,
Worshipping, knelt beside his stall;
Now Joseph, dream-led, guides the mule
Close by the shuttered wall.'

The singing faded as the cart turned into Keel Alley. Leaning close to the glass, Prudence heard one fading line—'*Herod's night-armies rake the town*'—and then nothing more.

It was very dark now. The shadows swallowed up the big candlestick. They could only see a solitary flame dancing on the darkness. As they watched, the flame flickered and sank, until it was only a bud of yellow, shrinking fast; then a needle's eye, then only a pinprick of light; and then no light at all except the glow of the wick, a single bright spark, fading into the darkness. Prudence, bending over it, smelt the last thread of smoke that floated on the quiet air.

Christmas was over.